掌握8大發音要訣!

LISTEN AND SPEAK OUT!

英語聽說超流暢

附MP3
音檔連結

Tim Stone
/ 著

聽說竅門・豁然大開
英檢・TOEIC 應試得高分!

笛藤出版

Introduction

前 言

　　在學習英語的過程中，老師為了提升學生學習的意願，總是會一字一句慢慢地、清楚地唸，雖然很容易就能聽清楚老師唸的英語，但久而久之，也形成我們聽 [慢速英語] 的習慣。可是一旦有機會跟外國人說話，或是在看電影、聽廣播、聽演講的場合中，英語完全不是這麼一回事，怎麼我們在課堂上所磨練出來的聽說功力，一下子完全無用武之地。人家打的是棒球，你學的偏偏是慢速壘球的技巧，真正上場比賽時，當然會灰頭土臉。

　　沒錯，英語是一種很有律動起伏的語言，我們因為受到母語—中文一字一義的影響，所以在英語的消音、連音方面不得不下點功夫。請注意，書中所有連音、消音、變音的要訣和音組的練習，無非是為了使說話更流暢。所以這些要訣不是用來強記，而是當說話速度加快時，自然而然產生的結果。

　　在了解本書 8 大要訣，112 條法則後，搭配 MP3 音檔，多聽多練習，相信英語聽力一定會突飛猛進，開口說英語時，也更能掌握美式英語的發音精髓，說出一口道地腔調。

註

a̸ ➡消音　a ➡弱化　aa ➡連音　ａ ➡變音
aa ➡同音只念一次　[ ] ➡ KK 音標

♪ **MP3 音檔請至下方連結下載：**

http://bit.ly/DTListen

（請注意網址大小寫區別。）

----

* MP3 英語發聲｜ Rachel Yang・Robert Fehr・Kronis
* 本書為《112 要訣！突破英聽力盲點》換封新版

Contents
目次

CHAPTER 1
口語連音七大超級常用字
- wanna, gonna, gotta, ya, yer, yers, cuz.

CHAPTER 2
[t]、[d]、[s]、[z] 與you(r)的微妙結合

CHAPTER 3
無傷大雅懶人音- 母音的弱化

CHAPTER 4
字尾加ed、ing 的發音要訣 與of常見片語組合

CHAPTER 7
高頻率連音組合

CHAPTER 8
實用經典表達句

CHAPTER 1

口語連音七大超級常用字

wanna gonna gotta ya yer yers cuz

當你和外國朋友在網路上聊天,或是當面交談,甚至聽美國流行歌曲時,三不五時就會聽到這些字,而規規矩矩學英語的我們,對它們是有點熟悉,卻又無法知道真正的意思,因為老師從來都不教這些。其實它們都是連音下的產物,非常普遍,在非正式的書寫上也經常使用。

want to
的連音變化

🔊 001

 → **wanna**
['wɑnə]

● 在美式英語中，[n]可說是[t]的頭號天敵，因為[n][t]在口腔中的發音位置相近，所以強勢的[n]會吃掉緊跟在後的[t]。在want to中，兩個t只要唸一次即可；不定詞to不具文字的意義，會弱化為[tə]；[n]造成[t]消音，[n]和[ə]連音，最終want to就演變成wanna這樣的口語說法了。(有關[n]遇上[t]，[t]被消音的規則，後面會陸續討論到。)

 Speak up

(1) Do you wanna go to the movies?	想去看電影嗎？
(2) I wanna finish eating first.	等我把東西吃完再說。
(3) Wanna play?	想玩嗎？
(4) You wanna swap?	你想要交換嗎？
(5) What do you wanna do?	你想做什麼？

•••●🐝

在口語的問句中，省略助動詞 do 或主詞 you 是很普遍的，視個人說話的習慣而有所不同。

11

2 going to
的連音變化

going to → gonna
[gənə]

● going to → gonna 跟 want to → wanna 有異曲同工之妙。go 弱化為 [gə]，ing 的 i，g 消音只留下[n]，to 弱化並受到[n]的影響只剩下[ə]，接著 [n] 和 [ə]連音，gonna 就這樣成形了。

🌸 *Speak up*

A: Are you gonna go to the party?

B: Yes, I'm gonna go very soon.

A: Who are you gonna go with?

B: I'm gonna go with my friends.

A: How are you gonna get there?

B: I'm gonna take my mom's car.

A: Is your mom gonna let you?

B: Don't worry, it's gonna be fine.

A：你會去參加那場派對嗎？

B：是啊，我馬上就要出發了。

A：有誰會跟你去嗎？

B：我的一些朋友會和我一起去參加。

A：你們要怎麼去？

B：我準備開我老媽的車去。

A：你媽會准嗎？

B：安啦！沒問題。

3 (have/has) got to 的連音變化

(have/has) got to → **gotta**
['gɑtə]

● "have/has got to" 意思等同於 "have/has to"（必須）。這是口語的表現方式，只會在很隨性的場合出現，最好避免用於正式談話或書寫上。有時說話速度一快，have 乾脆就省略，剩下 got to，兩個 t 只要唸一次，to 弱化成 [tə] 之後，gotta [gɑtə] 成了最終版。

😊 *Speak up*

(1) I gotta give him a call. 　　　我得打個電話給他。

(2) We gotta catch the train. 　　我們得趕上火車才行。

(3) You gotta see this! 　　　　這樣東西你一定得瞧瞧！

(4) They gotta sleep on the 　　他們今晚必須夜宿在火車上。
　　 train tonight.

(5) You gotta return those books! 你必須歸還那些書！

(6) He's gotta go to work now.   他現在得去上班了。

(7) She's gotta eat right now.   她現在得吃些東西才行。

(8) John's gotta stay home   John今晚必須待在家裡。
tonight.

(9) Our company's gotta hire   我們公司得多雇用10個員工
ten more workers.   才能忙得過來。

(10) Our team's gotta score one   我們這一隊必須多得一分才
more point to win!   能贏。

在以上有關 have/has gotta 的例句中，不知眼尖的你是否有發現，助動詞 have 通常會被省略，而 has 則會緊跟著單數主詞，形成「主詞's」的縮寫。然而，「主詞's」的形式和「主詞 is」的縮寫一模一樣，我們可以從後面接的詞性來辨別它是 "has" 還是 "is"。

you
的弱化

004

you ➔ **ya**
[jə]

● you 指的是和你對話的人，既然都已經面對面了，you [ju] 當然也就逃不過被弱化成 ya [jə] 的命運囉！

🐛 *Speak up*

. . . .

(1) I'll phone ya.   我再call你喔！

(2) See ya later!   再見！

(3) Told ya so!   早就跟你說了！

(4) Catch ya later!   再見！

(5) Nice to see ya!   真高興見到你！幸會！幸會！

your you're 的弱化

■))005

your / you're → yer
[jɚ]

● your 和 you're 的 ou 在唸快時，都會被弱化，形成了 yer 的音。有時在書寫時就直接寫成yer。

🌸 Speak up

ⓐ your [juɚ] → yer [jɚ]

(1) What's yer name?   你叫什麼名字？

(2) Is this yer car?   這是你的車嗎？

(3) It's not yer fault.   不是你的錯。

ⓑ you're [juɚ] → yer [jɚ]

(1) Yer funny !   你很好笑哎！

(2) Thanks! Yer my hero.   謝謝！你真是我的英雄！

(3) If yer busy, I'll call later.   如果你忙的話，我等一下再打給你好了。

yours
的弱化

🔊 006

yours → **yers**
[jɚs]

● yours 的 ou 在唸快時會被弱化，形成了 yers 的音。yours 的 s 原本是發 [z] 的音，但為求說話方便，會以 [s] 輕輕帶過。yers 的寫法常出現在非正式的書寫中。

🌼 *Speak up*

(1) Is this camera yers?　　　這台相機是你的嗎？

(2) These slippers are yers.　　這雙拖鞋是你的。

(3) My phone is ugly. Yers is cute!　　我的手機醜斃了。你的才可愛勒！

17

7 because 的變化

be̸cause → CUZ
[kəz]

● because 只是個連接詞，短短帶過即可，所以 be 被消音，cause [kɔz] 的 au 弱化，便成為簡潔的 [kəz] 了，通常會直接寫成 cuz。

🌸 *Speak up*

(1) She's angry cuz I lied to her. 她因為我說謊而大發雷霆。

(2) Cuz I said so, that's why. 因為我說的算，就這樣。

(3) I need an umbrella cuz it's raining. 因為外面在下雨，所以我需要一把傘。

(4) I didn't go out last night cuz I was tired. 因為我昨晚太累了，所以沒出去。

(5) I like you cuz you're honest. 因為你很誠實，所以我很喜歡你。

CHAPTER 1 實況對話總複習
Practice Speaking Challenge!

▼ Jenny 打電話找 Joe

Jenny: Hello? Is Joe there?

Joe: This is Joe. Hi Jenny!

Jenny: Hi Joe. How are ____?

Joe: Fine, and ____?

Jenny: Not bad, thanks! What are ____ doing

tonight?

Joe: Nothing, I _____ go out. What are _____ plans?

Jenny: I'm _____ be in a festival! You _____ come!

Joe: A festival? Really? I love festivals!

Jenny: Yes, a ghost festival! Hee hee!

Joe: Oh, really? What are _____ wear?

Jenny: I'm _____ wear a white dress and white

make-up.

Joe: Oh! What do_____ do there?

Jenny: I _____ dance and scream for one hour!

Joe: Oh! What time does the festival start?

Jenny: The festival starts at midnight.

Joe: Oh! It's eleven p.m. now. Are _____ go

there soon?

Jenny: Yeah! So, do you _____ come?

Joe: No, not anymore.

Jenny: _____ kidding. Why not?

Joe: _____ now I'm too scared!

Aɴswer Keys
Chapter 1 Practice Speaking Challenge!

▼ Jenny 打電話找 Joe

Jenny: Hello? Is Joe there?

哈囉！Joe在嗎？

Joe: This is Joe. Hi Jenny!

我就是。嗨，Jenny！

Jenny: Hi Joe. How are ya?!

哈囉，Joe！你好嗎？

Joe: Fine, and ya?

很好啊，你呢？

Jenny: Not bad, thanks! What are ya doing tonight?

還不錯啊，謝謝！你今晚有事嗎？

Joe: Nothing, I wanna go out. What are yer plans?

沒有耶，可是我好想出去晃晃。你今晚有什麼計畫嗎？

Jenny: I'm gonna be in a festival! You gotta come!

我要去參加一個派對活動！你一定得來才行！

Joe: A festival? Really? I love festivals!

派對活動？真的嗎？我最喜歡派對了！

Jenny: Yes, a ghost festival! Hee hee!

是啊！今晚活動的主題是鬼魅總動員！嘿嘿！

Joe: Oh, really? What are ya gonna wear?

喔，真的嗎？那你要打扮成什麼？

Jenny: I'm gonna wear a white dress and white make-up.

我要穿白衣，然後化慘白的死人妝。

Joe: Oh! What do ya gotta do there?

喔！那你打算在那裡做什麼？

Jenny: I gotta dance and scream for one hour!

我打算在那裡跳舞、狂叫一小時！

Joe: Oh! What time does the festival start?

嗯！派對什麼時候開始呢？

Jenny: The festival starts at midnight.

午夜才開始。

Joe: Oh! It's eleven p.m. now. Are ya gonna go there soon?

哦！現在已經晚上11點了，你該很快就要出發了吧？

Jenny: Yeah! So, do you wanna come?

對啊！你要參加嗎？

Joe: No, not anymore.

我看還是不要好了。

Jenny: Yer kidding. Why not?

你開玩笑的吧。為什麼不要？

Joe: Cuz now I'm too scared!

因為現在光講我就已經嚇得半死了。

CHAPTER 2

[t]、[d]、[s]、[z]與you(r) 的微妙結合

在句子中，you除了常被弱化成ya，也常和前一個單字的尾音發生連音的變化喔。

8 尾音 t + you = tcha

~t you → tcha
[tʃə]

● 常在電影中聽到 "What about you?" 這句話,其中,what 的 h 常被省略而唸成 wat,about 的尾音 t 則和 you 形成連音 tcha,所以你實際上聽到的是 "wataboutcha"。把說話速度調快連起來唸唸看,你也會發出漂亮的音喔。【註】這邊的 tch [tʃ] 因為前後母音的關係,會稍稍強化成 dch [dʒ],請參考第73條要訣。

🌸 *Speak up*

....

(1) What about you?
    What aboutcha?

你勒?

(2) Got you!
    Gotcha!

瞭了/哈哈!騙到你了!/
逮到你了吧!(此句有多種
意思,要視對話的內容而定)

(3) Nice to meet you.
    Nice to meetcha.

很高興見到你。

(4) Don't you want to go?
    Don'tcha want to go?

你不去嗎?

(5) Can't you study some other time?
Can'tcha study some other time?

你不能找其他時間讀書嗎？

(6) I always think about you.
I always think aboutcha.

我總是無時無刻想著你。

(7) You called me, didn't you?
You called me, didn'tcha?

你有打電話給我，對不對？

(8) Sorry, I thought you were someone else.
Sorry, I thoughtcha were someone else.

真抱歉，我剛誤認為你是另外一個人。

(9) Didn't you eat yet?
Didn'tcha eat yet?

你還沒吃飯啊？

(10) Why won't you call me?
Why won'tcha call me?

你為什麼不會打電話給我？

i ALWAYS THiNK ABOUT YOU.

9 尾音d+you =dcha

◀))010

~d you → **dcha**
[dʒə]

● 尾音d和you形成連音dcha。dcha [dʒə] 是 tcha [tʃə] 的有聲版本，先把口型固定住，再從喉嚨送氣發聲，就可以唸出漂亮的音了。

😊 *Speak up*

(1) What di**d you** do?　　　　　你做了什麼？
　　What di**dcha** do?

(2) Coul**d you** get that for me?　　你可以幫我拿這東西嗎？
　　Coul**dcha** get that for me?

(3) Di**d you** see that?　　　　　你有看到嗎？
　　Di**dcha** see that?

(4) Woul**d you** please help me?　　你可以幫我個忙嗎？
　　Woul**dcha** please help me?

(5) How di**d you** do that?　　　　你怎麼辦到的？
　　How di**dcha** do that?

10 尾音s + you = scha

~s you → scha
[ʃə]

● s與弱化的you[jə]結合，形成連音scha[ʃə]。scha[ʃə]的音很像[噓…]，唯一不同的是嘴唇不用太翹，適度就好。

🌸 *Speak up*

. . . .

(1) I'll miss you.　　　　　　　　　我會很想你的。
　　I'll misscha.

(2) Bless you.　　　　　　　　　　祝福你。(對方打噴嚏時，
　　Blesscha.　　　　　　　　　　可派上用場的一句話)

(3) She won't go unless you go.　　除非你去，否則她是不會去
　　She won't go unlesscha go.　　的。

"Bless You!" 當有人打噴嚏時，常常聽到這句話。為啥人家鼻子不舒服，需要別人給個祝福呢？這還不是普通的祝福喔！這句原本應該是"God bless you!" —打噴嚏時，要請神來祝福你，這夠嚴重吧！其實它是有典故的：據說，當你打噴嚏的時候，是靈魂最脆弱的時候，它會飄飄然地跟著噴嚏從鼻子噴出去，這時躲在一旁的魔鬼就會趁機抓走你的靈魂，所以只要旁邊的人說一聲"God bless you!"，就可以嚇阻魔鬼下手取你靈魂的行動。所以下次有人打噴嚏時，你也可以幫他一把，說聲「Bless you.」，幫他把靈魂抓回來。

尾音Z+your =zcher

🔊012

~z your → zcher
[ʒɚ]

●很多單字如 was, lose, use, news，雖然是以字母s或se結尾，但發的卻是不折不扣的 [z] 音。一旦 [z] 碰上 your 就會形成連音 zcher[ʒɚ]。zch[ʒ] 的發音介於注音的 [ㄖ] 跟 dch[dʒ] 之間，發 zch[ʒ] 音時，會有種空氣在嘴裡打轉，舌頭前段麻麻的奇妙感覺。

🌸 *Speak up*

(1) It was your job, not mine.　　　　這是你該做的工作，不要留
　　 It wazcher job, not mine.　　　　給我收拾爛攤子。
(2) That was your fault.　　　　　　　都是你的錯。
　　 That wazcher fault.
(3) I don't wanna lose you.　　　　　　我不想失去你。
　　 I don't wanna lozcha.

(4) Where's your wallet?　　　　你的皮夾在哪裡？
Where'zcher wallet?

(5) How's your family?　　　　你的家人還好嗎？
How'zcher family?

(6) Can I use your laptop?　　　可以用一下你的筆記型電腦
Can I uzcher laptop?　　　　嗎？

(7) Which bike is yours?　　　　你的腳踏車是哪一輛？
Which bike izchers?

CHAPTER 2 實況對話總複習
Practice Speaking Challenge!

Dennis wanders into an electronics store.
A saleswoman approaches him.
丹尼斯走進一家電器用品專賣店，一位女售貨員走過來招呼他。

Saleswoman: Hello, can I assist you with something?

哈囉！請問有什麼需要服務的地方嗎？

Dennis: Yes, I'm looking for a gift for my son's
graduation.

我想挑個東西送我兒子當畢業禮物。

Saleswoman: Oh! What does your son want?

喔！你兒子有什麼特別想要的東西嗎？

Dennis: Well, I'm not sure. He's usually very picky.

嗯，我不太確定他喜歡什麼，他通常很挑剔。

Saleswoman: Would you like to see some toys?

挑個玩具送他如何？

Dennis: No, this year he's too old for toys.

不好吧，他已經過了玩玩具的年齡了。

Saleswoman: Does your son like music?

那麼你兒子喜歡聽音樂嗎？

Dennis: Yes, but you don't have CDs here.

喜歡啊，但你們這裡好像沒賣CD。

Saleswoman: What about this camera phone?

那這支照相手機如何？

Dennis: That's a good idea! What's your price?

好主意！這支手機要多少錢呢？

Saleswoman: It's yours for three thousand dollars.

只要三千元這支手機就是你的了。

Dennis: I'll take it. Could you wrap it up for me?

那我就買這支手機了。可以幫我包裝嗎？

Saleswoman: Sure, I'll wrap it in tissue paper.

可以啊，我會用棉紙幫您包起來。

Dennis: Wait! Can I take a picture of you with the

phone?

等等！我能用這支手機幫你拍張照嗎？

Saleswoman: Sure. Why would you want a picture

of me?

可以啊！但為什麼要我的照片呢？

Dennis: Not for me! For my son! You are my son's type!

不是我要的啦！照片是給我兒子的！因為你恰巧是

我兒子喜歡的類型！

CHAPTER 3

無傷大雅懶人音-母音的弱化

不影響句子意思的單字，其母音會輕輕發[ə]帶過，甚至接近消音的程度！（通常出現在 be 動詞、介系詞、連接詞、代名詞等，在句中較沒實質意義的字上。）

SO
在句中音變弱

SO

🔊 014

[sə]

● 在不特別強調 so 的情況下，so 會輕輕帶過唸成 [sə]。

🌼 *Speak up*

(1) It's so nice of you to come.　你能大駕光臨真是太好了。

(2) What's so funny about that?　那有什麼好笑的啊？

(3) Don't be so nervous.　別太緊張。

(4) She's my sister, so be nice to her.　她是我妹，所以要對她好一點喔。

(5) I worked hard, so you should pay me.　因為我很賣力工作，所以你要付我薪水。

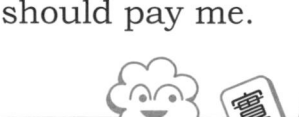

A: Honey, why did you turn off the lights? It's so dark!
親愛的，你為什麼把燈關掉？很暗耶！

B: I turned the light off so our dinner can be romantic.
把燈關了，這樣我們的晚餐就會變得很浪漫呀！

A: You're so silly. Now I can't see my dinner or you.
你很傻耶，現在我連你和晚餐的食物都看不到了，怎麼浪漫得起來。

for
在句中音變弱

for
[fɚ]

● 在不特別強調 for 的情況下，for 會輕輕帶過，弱化成 [fɚ]。

🌸 *Speak up*

(1) Thanks for the gift.　　　　　謝謝你送我禮物。

(2) I would do anything for you.　我願意為你犧牲一切。

(3) For sure!　　　　　　　　　當然！

(4) The book is for you.　　　　　這本書送你。

(5) Is this key for your house?　這是你家的鑰匙嗎？

A: Wake up! You're late for your appointment!
　　起床！你約會要遲到了！

B: Oh, I over-slept! I slept for fifteen hours!
　　呃，我睡過頭了！ 我睡了15個小時！

A: What are you waiting for? Get up!
　　那你還等什麼？趕快起來啊！

14

or
在句中音變弱

or
[ɚ]

● or [ɔr] 的母音弱化，發音由原來的 [ɔr] → [ɚ]。

🌸 *Speak up*

. . . .

(1) Trick or treat!   不給糖，就搗蛋！

(2) Do you want to sit inside or   你要坐裡面還外面？
　　outside?

(3) Is this drink mine or yours?   這是我的飲料還是你的？

(4) Is your sister tall or short?   你妹妹是高還是矮？

(5) Are you coming or not?   你到底要不要來？

A: Honey, shall we go home by bus or by taxi?
　　親愛的，我們該坐公車、還是搭計程車回家？

B: Believe it or not, we spent all our money.
　　不瞞你說，我們已經把所有的錢花光了。

A: Oh. Shall we walk home or run home?
　　喔！那我們是要走回家、還是跑回家？

37

at
在句中音變弱

at
[ət]

● 在句中，原本得誇大口型來唸的 at [æt] 變成了含蓄的 [ət]。

🌸 Speak up

(1) I'll see you at 10 p.m.　　　　晚上10點見囉。

(2) I like swimming at night.　　　我喜歡晚上游泳。

(3) Stop looking at me.　　　　　　別一直盯著我看。

(4) Sorry, she's not at home.　　　很抱歉，她不在家。

(5) Let's meet at the restaurant.　我們就在餐廳見囉。

實 戰 對 話

A: I saw a big black snake at the park at lunch today.
　　我今天在公園吃午餐時看到一條大黑蛇。

B: Oh! Did it lunge at you?
　　喔！牠有撲向你嗎？

A: No. It looked at my lunch, then it hissed at me.
　　沒有。牠看了看我的午餐，然後對我發出嘶嘶的警示聲。

 **and**
在句中變成 ’n

[ən]

● and後面若是接子音開頭的字，通常and的a會被弱化，d被消音。and 的d被消音後，唸起來是不是很像在唸字母的 N 呢？所以有時候你會看到 「and」變身為「'n」的懶人寫法。

 *Speak up*

....

(1) At the zoo I saw lions and monkeys and bears.
At the zoo I saw lions 'n monkeys 'n bears.

我在動物園有看到獅子和猴子和熊。

(2) He asked me out over and over again.
He asked me out over 'n over again.

他一直想約我出去。

(3) Let's have ham and eggs for breakfast.
Let's have ham 'n eggs for breakfast.

我們早餐吃火腿蛋吧。

39

(4) Would you like cream and
sugar in your coffee?

Would you like cream 'n
sugar in your coffee?

你咖啡要加奶精跟糖嗎？

(5) The secret is between you
and me.

The secret is between you 'n
me.

這個秘密只有你知我知。

(6) You'd better tell Dad and
Mom.

You'd better tell Dad 'n
Mom.

你最好老實跟爸媽說。

A: Can you get me one black tea and a piece of cake?
可以給我一杯紅茶和一塊蛋糕嗎？
B: That will be one hundred and fifty NT.
總共150元。
A: What? I thought you and me were good friends!
什麼？要付錢？我以為我們是朋友勒！

to
在句中音變弱

to
[tə]

● to 和 so, for, and 一樣都有被弱化的傾向，輕輕以 [tə] 帶過就行囉。

🌸 *Speak up*

. . . .

(1) Happy Birthday to you.   祝你生日快樂。

(2) That's easy for you to say.   你說得倒輕鬆。

(3) You should tell me what to do. 你應該告訴我怎麼做。

(4) Aren't you going to Hawaii   你不是要去夏威夷度蜜月嗎？
     for your honeymoon?

(5) Remember to email me.   要記得email給我喔。

A: Mom, my favorite TV show is going to start soon.
    媽咪，我最愛的電視節目就要開始播了。

B: Son, I'm sorry. You have to go to bed soon.
    兒子啊，很抱歉你不行看，你必須上床睡覺了。

A: Mom? Can I bring the TV to bed with me?
    媽咪？那我可以把電視搬到床上嗎？

into
在句中唸成 [ˈɪntə]

into
[ˈɪntə]

🔊 020

● into 是由 to 延伸出來的字，當然弱化的原則也是比照 to 了。

🌸 *Speak up*

(1) The caterpillar changed into a butterfly!　　毛毛蟲變蝴蝶了！

(2) The cat jumped into the bathtub.　　貓咪跳進浴缸裡去了。

(3) Look into my eyes.　　看著我的眼睛。

(4) She's really into herself.　　她真的很自戀。

(5) I got into trouble after school.　　我在放學後闖禍了。

A: Knock, knock! Did you fall into the toilet?
　　叩叩！你掉到馬桶裡去了嗎？
B: No, I dropped my phone into the toilet.
　　不是啦，我手機掉到馬桶裡了啦。
A: I'll go into the kitchen and get some gloves.
　　我到廚房去拿手套。

19

are
快唸變成 [ɚ]

are
[ɚ]

◀》021

● are 唸快一點就變成 er [ɚ] 了，尤其是當寫成「主詞 're」時！還記得第 5 個要訣中提到 you're 會唸成 yer 嗎？其實就是這個道理。

🌼 *Speak up*

(1) They are here with us.　　　　　　他們在這裡陪伴我們。
They're here with us.

(2) Birds are hard to spot.　　　　　　鳥類的行蹤很難掌控。
Birds're hard to spot.

(3) Why are you looking at me?　　　　你為什麼一直盯著我看？
Why're you looking at me?

(4) We are your new neighbors.　　　　我們是你的新鄰居。
We're your new neighbors.

(5) Where are you from?　　　　　　　你從哪個國家(地方)來的？
Where're you from?

A: Mom? Are you going shopping soon?
媽咪？你是不是要去買東西了？

B: Why? Are you kids hungry already?
怎麼了？小朋友你們肚子餓啊？

A: No, we are bored. Can we go with you?
沒有啦，只是覺得很無聊，我們可不可以跟你一起去逛街呢？

in
在句中怎麼唸？

in
[ən]

🔊022

● in 的 i [ɪ] 弱化成 [ə]。

 *Speak up*

. . . .

(1) Come on in.　　　　　　　　請進。

(2) Call me back in ten minutes.　十分鐘後打電話給我。

(3) Are you two in love?　　　　　你們兩個是不是在談戀愛？

(4) I found a spider in my shoe.　我在鞋子裡發現一隻蜘蛛。

(5) Throw it in the garbage can.　把它丟到垃圾桶去。

A: Mmm. This pepper tastes good in the rice.
嗯…這個胡椒配飯好好吃喔。

B: What? I didn't put pepper in the rice.
什麼？我飯裡沒放胡椒啊。

A: Hey! There are rat droppings in my rice! Ew!
嘿！這是老鼠屎！噁！

but
輕輕唸成 [bət]

but

🔊 023

[bət]

● 因為 but 是連接詞的關係，所以會輕輕以 [bət] 帶過。

🌸 *Speak up*

. . . .

(1) She says she likes me, but she never calls me.

她說她喜歡我，但從沒打電話給我過。

(2) He's tired, but he's happy.

雖然很累，但他還是樂此不疲。

(3) I'm tired, but I can't sleep.

雖然很累，但我還是無法入眠。

(4) But it's not true!

但是那不是真的！

(5) I'll go to the tea shop, but only for an hour.

我會去茶坊，但只會在那裡待一小時。

A: I can go swimming, but only for ten minutes.
　我可以去游泳，但是只游十分鐘喔。
B: But I thought you loved swimming!
　我還以為你很喜歡游泳勒！
A: I do love swimming, but your pool stinks!
　我是喜歡啊，但你游泳池的水好臭！

45

22 冠詞 **a** 的練習

a
[ə]

● 冠詞 a 後面接的是子音開頭的可數名詞。下次仔細聽，有些美國人會把 a 唸成字母 a [e] 的發音喔，不過唸成 [ə] 或 [e] 是看個人喜好而定，兩種唸法都很美式。

 *Speak up*

....

(1) Can I ask you a question?　　　我能問你個問題嗎？

(2) I'll have a glass of water.　　　請給我一杯水。

(3) I need a bit more sleep.　　　我需要多一點睡眠。

(4) She feels a little cold.　　　她覺得有點冷。

(5) Try a piece of bread.　　　來嚐塊麵包如何。

23 冠詞 **an** 的練習

an
[ən]

● 冠詞 an 後面接的是母音開頭的可數名詞。

🌸 *Speak up*

(1) I'll see you in an hour or so.　　一個小時後見。

(2) I bought an orange skirt.　　我買了件橘色的裙子。

(3) Did you see an apple on the table?　　你在桌上有看到一顆蘋果嗎？

(4) The bus comes in half an hour.　　公車半小時後就來了。

(5) He's an honest man.　　他為人很誠實。

CHAPTER 3 實況對話總複習

Practice Speaking Challenge! so, for, or, at, and, to, into, are, in, but, a, an.

▼ **A child and a woman meet at the beach.**
一個小孩看到一個女人在沙灘上找東西。

Child: Hi, excuse me, _____?

Adult: I'm _____ my ring. I lost it!

Child: Too bad! Is it _____?

Adult: It's _____! Very expensive!

Child: Oh! _____?

Adult: I don't know. Can you help me find it?

Child: Sure, _____. It's so hot.

Adult: You search there _____ I'll search here

Child: OK... Hey! I found _____.

Adult: Really? It's _____. What is it?

Child: _____ the color! It's ____ gold coin!

Adult: Great! _____ your pocket.

Child: Hey! I found a 10NT coin! Hee hee!

Adult: Really? You have very good eyes.

Child: _____ is fun! I found many things!

Adult: Yes,_____ find my ring?

Child: Actually, I found your ring ten minutes ago.

Adult: Really? Where? _____? _____!

Child: _____. The ring is on your towel!

Aɴsᴡᴇʀ Kᴇʏs

Chapter 3 Practice Speaking Challenge!

▼ A child and a woman meet at the beach.
一個小孩看到一個女人在沙灘上找東西。

Child: Hi, excuse me, what are you looking for?

嗨，請問你在找什麼？

Adult: I'm looking for my ring. I lost it!

我在找我的戒指，因為我把它弄丟了！

Child: Too bad! Is it expensive or cheap?

真糟糕！是貴還是便宜的戒指？

Adult: It's a wedding ring! Very expensive!

是一只結婚戒指！很昂貴的！

Child: Oh! What are you going to do?

喔！那你要怎麼辦？

Adult: I don't know. Can you help me find it?

不曉得。你能幫我找嗎？

Child: Sure, but only for an hour or so. It's so hot.

好，但我只幫你找一小時喔，因為好熱。

Adult: You search there and I'll search here.

你到那邊找找，我在這裡找。

Child: OK... Hey! I found something in the sand

好…嘿！我在沙子裡找到了一個東西！

Adult: Really? It's so shiny. What is it?

真的嗎？這閃閃發光的東西到底是什麼？

Child: Look at the color! It's a gold coin!

依顏色看來應該是一枚金幣！

Adult: Great! Put it into your pocket.

太好了！趕快把它放進你口袋。

Child: Hey! I found a 10NT coin! Hee hee!

嘿！我還找到了一枚十元硬幣！ 嘻嘻！

Adult: Really? You have very good eyes.

真的嗎？ 你的眼力很好喔。

Child: Looking for things is fun! I found many things!

找東西真好玩！我找到好多東西喔！

Adult: Yes, but can you find my ring?

嗯，但你能幫忙找找我的戒指嗎？

Child: Actually, I found your ring ten minutes ago.

事實上，我十分鐘前就已經找到你的戒指了。

Adult: Really? Where? In the sand? Give it to me!

真的嗎？哪裡？在沙子裡嗎？趕快給我啊！

Child: You are so funny. The ring is on your towel!

你很好笑耶，戒指就在你的毛巾上啊！

CHAPTER 4

字尾加ed、ing的發音要訣 與of常見片語組合

規則動詞加ed時，動詞本身尾音不同，後面ed所發的音也會有所不同。而動詞後面加上ing時，ing的尾音會變得非常地微弱。此章也列出of常見片語，並精解can、can't發音的差異，以增加讀者辨音的能力。

24

動詞 + ed，
ed 唸 [d]
（動詞以母音或
有聲子音結尾）

■》027

played [pled]
learned [lɜnd]

● 規則動詞變過去式或過去分詞時，字尾會加 ed。為方便發音，ed 的唸法會隨著單字尾音而有所不同。以下為歸類的三種情況：

(a) 當單字以母音或有聲子音結尾時，加上的 ed 會唸成有聲版的 [d]。
(b) 當單字以無聲子音結尾時，加上的 ed 會唸成無聲版的 [t]。
(c) 當單字是以 [t] 或 [d] 結尾時，加上的 ed 會唸成 [ɪd]。

🌸 *Speak up*

當單字以母音或有聲子音結尾時，加上的 ed 會唸成有聲版的 [d]。

(1) My mom and I played tennis this morning.　今天早上我跟我媽在打網球。

(2) Have you ordered lunch yet?　你訂午餐了沒？

(3) We cheered for the home team.　我們支持地主隊。

(4) I learned how to drive when I was twenty.　我二十歲時開始學開車。

(5) I called you cuz I was bored.　因為很無聊所以我才打電話找你聊天。

1. 若 -ed[d] 後面接的是子音開頭的單字，[d] 的發聲會變得非常微弱，有時甚至會到達消音的地步。當你說話速度一快，這個現象會自然而然發生。
2. 若 -ed[d] 後面接的是母音開頭的單字，[d] 會和隨後的母音形成連音，也就是一氣呵成，不斷音的意思。（請參考Chapter 5）
3. 若 -ed[d] 後面接的是子音 [d] 開頭的單字，兩個 [d] 只要發一次音即可。

25 動詞 + ed，
ed 唸 [t]
（動詞以無聲子音結尾）

talked [tɔkt]

⏹))028

*Speak up*

當單字以無聲子音結尾時，加上的 ed 會唸成無聲版的 [t]。

- -

(1) Have you talked to him about the project yet? 　你跟他談這個企劃了沒？

(2) He dressed nicely for the party. 　他為了參加這個派對而特地打扮一番。

(3) I walked the dog this morning. 　我早上有去溜狗。

(4) Is the door locked? 　門有上鎖嗎？

(5) We camped in the mountain last night. 　昨晚我們在山上露營。

- -

1. 若 -ed[t] 後面接的是子音開頭的單字，[t] 的發聲會變得非常微弱，有時甚至會到達消音的地步。當你說話速度一快，這個現象會自然而然發生。

2. 若 -ed[t] 後面接的是母音開頭的單字，[t] 會和隨後的母音形成連音，也就是一氣呵成，不斷音的意思。（請參考 Chapter 5）

3. 若 -ed[t] 後面接的是子音 [t] 開頭的單字，兩個 [t] 只要發一次音即可。

26 動詞+ed，
ed唸 [ɪd]
（動詞以[t]或[d]結尾）

🔊 029

decided [dɪ'saɪdɪd]

🌸 Speak up

當單字是以 [t] 或 [d] 結尾時，加上的 ed 會唸成 [ɪd]。

- -

(1) I've decided to ignore him.　我已經決定不理他了。
(2) I wanted to go but I fell asleep!　我其實很想去，但我睡著了！
(3) The movie lasted two hours.　這部電影長達兩個小時。
(4) She trusted him, and he cheated.　她這麼信任他，他竟然還出軌。
(5) You're invited to my birthday!　歡迎參加我的生日派對！

- -

1. 若 -ed[ɪd] 後面接的是子音開頭的單字，[d] 的發聲會變得非常微弱，有時甚至會到達消音的地步。當你說話速度一快，這個現象會自然而然發生。
2. 若 -ed[ɪd] 後面接的是母音開頭的單字，[d] 會和隨後的母音形成連音，也就是一氣呵成，不斷音的意思。（請參考 Chapter 5）
3. 若 -ed[ɪd] 後面接的是子音 [d] 開頭的單字，兩個 [d] 只要發一次音即可。

27

-ing
變-in'

~ing [ɪn]

● 說話速度飆快時，"ing"[ɪŋ] 中的 i [ɪ] 會被弱化，[ŋ] 變成 [n]，成為[ɪn] 的唸法。這就是為什麼有時動詞後面加 ing，g 會被省略。比如說 What's happenin'? 等等。在非正式書寫時，ing 通常會寫成 in'。

🌸 *Speak up*

(1) What's happenin'?	你怎麼了？
(2) What's goin' on?	怎麼了？
(3) What ya doin'?	你在做什麼？(口語中be動詞被省略是很常見的。)
(4) I'm watchin' a movie.	我在看電影。
(5) I'm gettin' hungry.	我有點餓了。
(6) Where are you goin'?	你要去哪裡？
(7) Are you kiddin' me?	你該不會是在跟我開玩笑吧！
(8) I'm catchin' a cold.	我感冒了。

28 單字中的 to 輕輕唸

🔊 031

to
[tə]

● 當 to 不在單字的重音節時，會輕輕帶過唸成 [tə]。在單字中，輕輕帶過且身段優美的 to，請跟著 MP3 溫柔地聽。

🌸 *Speak up*

. . . .

(1) Sorry, I have plans for tonight.　　抱歉，我今晚有事。

(2) I think it's going to rain today.　　我想今天會下雨。

(3) Are you busy tomorrow?　　你明天忙嗎？

(4) They will be together forever.　　他們會永遠在一起。

(5) I need to make a to-do list.　　我需要列一張工作清單。

58

29 of 在片語中變弱並連音

of

[əv]

032

● 因為 of[ɑv] 是介系詞的關係，也是輕輕帶過就行了，所以 of 就會被弱化成 [əv]，以下列了幾組常和 of 搭配的片語組合，也是會話中耳熟能詳的，多唸幾遍，你的 of 發音和聽力會更完美喔！

1 a couple of 幾個

a couple of ➡ akablav [ə'kʌbləv]

couple 的 [p] 在這裡有稍稍唸成 [b] 的傾向，但還沒到達 100% 有聲 [b] 的程度。

Speak up

(1) I've seen this movie a couple of times.	這部電影我已經看過好幾遍了。
(2) I only have a couple of vacation days left.	我只剩幾天特別假可用而已。
(3) Can I borrow a couple of dollars?	可以借我一點錢嗎？

(4) You two are acting like a couple of idiots! 你們兩個的行為舉止簡直跟笨蛋沒兩樣！

(5) Just give me a couple of minutes. 給我幾分鐘的時間。

(6) He looks like he drank a couple of beers. 看他的樣子好像是喝了幾瓶啤酒。

② a lot of 很多

 a lot of ➡ aladav [ə'lɑdəv]

[t] 音夾在兩個母音中間，所以被強化成比 [有聲 d] 來得輕快的 [彈舌音 d] 。

🌸 *Speak up*

(1) I have a lot of work to do. 我有很多工作要做。

(2) He has a lot of money. 他很有錢。

(3) It's important to drink a lot of water. 多喝水很重要。

(4) There aren't a lot of things we can do for her right now. 我們現在沒辦法幫她什麼忙。

(5) I don't have a lot of time. 我時間不多。

(6) There's a lot of soda in the refrigerator. 冰箱裡有很多汽水。

3 the rest of 其餘的

the res<u>t</u> of ➜ the resdav [ðə'rɛsdəv]

這邊的 [t] 被後面緊接的母音強化成 [d]。

🌸 Speak up

(1) The rest of the people went home early.　　其餘的人早早就回家了。

(2) I'll love her for the rest of my life.　　我會愛她一輩子。

(3) You can have the rest of my cake.　　你可以吃我剩下的蛋糕。

(4) Here's the rest of the money I owe you.　　這是我最後欠你的錢。

(5) Can I have the rest of the beer?　　剩下的啤酒我可以喝嗎？

4 a piece of 一片

a pie<u>c</u>e of ➜ apizav [ə'pizəv]

piece [pis] 中的 [s] 因受到後面 of [əv] 母音的影響，會被強化為 [z]。

🌸 Speak up

(1) Can you give me a piece of cake?　　能給我一片蛋糕嗎？

(2) There's a piece of pie left on the kitchen counter.

廚房流理台有塊派。

(3) I want to give her a piece of my mind.

我會清楚地跟她表達我的想法的。

(4) Would you like a piece of my cookie?

你要來片餅乾嗎？

(5) There's a piece of spinach stuck in your teeth.

有塊菠菜渣卡在你的牙縫裡。

5 some of the 其中一些

some of the ➡ somav the [ˈsʌməvðə]

some 和 of 要一氣呵成連起來唸。

😊 *Speak up*

(1) Some of the girls at the party were very pretty.

派對上有些女生很美。

(2) I saw some of the paintings by Michelangelo.

我看到了一些米開朗基羅的畫作。

(3) Some of the things you said yesterday were inappropriate.

你昨天說的一些事並不是很恰當。

(4) I hardly use some of the programs on my computer.

電腦上有一些程式我幾乎很少使用。

(5) Try some of the chicken, it tastes good!

嚐嚐這些雞肉，很好吃喔！

6 one of 其中一個

one of ➡ wanav ['wʌnəv]

one of 要一氣呵成連起來唸。

🌸 Speak up

(1) He's one of the best students in this class.

他是這個班上最好的學生之一。

(2) She's one of the prettiest girls I have ever seen.

她是我見過最美的女孩之一。

(3) I'll buy one of the computers in this store.

我打算在這家店買電腦。

(4) One of the houses on this street is haunted.

這條街上的其中一間屋子鬧鬼。

(5) One of our neighbors won the lottery!

我們其中一個鄰居中了樂透！

7 in front of 在前面

in front of ➡ infrandav [ən'frʌndəv]

還記得我們第一章談到說話速度快時，緊跟在 [n] 後面的 [t] 會很自然地被消音嗎？於是在 in front of 中就形成 [t] 消音、子音 [n] 和母音 [ə] 子母連音的結果了。但記住，若有人說話時，[t] 沒有消音，反倒是和後面的 [ə] 連音時，也不用覺得太訝異，他可能只是說話速度比較慢，有時間將 [t] 發出來，而 [t] 因為後面接母音 [ə]，所以強化成 [d]。

🌸 *Speak up*

(1) She was standing in front of 她站在房屋前面。
    the house.

(2) Whose red car is in front of 是誰的紅色車子停在我家
    my house?   前面？

(3) He spends too much time in 他花太多時間在看電視上。
    front of the television.

(4) There's someone waiting in 有人在你辦公室前面等你。
    front of your office.

(5) Stop walking in front of me. 別老是擋在我前面。

(6) I almost hit the bike in front 我差點撞到前面的腳踏車。
    of me.

🌸 the bottom of 在底部

the bottom of ➡ the badamav
                    [ðə'bɑdəməv]

仔細聽 MP3 上外籍老師唸的，你會發現 bottom 的 [t] 被偷偷唸成 [d]
了。因為無聲的 tt 被兩個母音包圍，所以會稍稍強化為 [彈舌音 d]。

🌸 *Speak up*

(1) It's the bottom of the ninth 已經到了九局下半。
    inning.

(2) You'll find it in the bottom 你會在抽屜底部找到它。
    of the drawer.

(3) Sometimes the best apples are at the bottom of the barrel.   有時最好的蘋果會被裝在桶子的最底部。

(4) The door to the basement is at the bottom of the stairs.   通往地下室的門在樓梯的最底部。

(5) I'll get to the bottom of this mystery!   我會把這個秘密查個水落石出的！

(6) A home run in the bottom of the ninth!   九局下半的全壘打！

⑨ a bunch of 一群、一堆

a bunch of ➡ abantchav [əˈbʌntʃəv]

bunch 和 of 要一氣呵成連起來唸。

🐝 *Speak up*

(1) There were a bunch of people at the party.   派對裡有一堆人。

(2) A bunch of money went down the drain.   一堆錢都被揮霍光了。

(3) That movie was a bunch of trash.   那部電影爛透了。

(4) I'm going out with a bunch of friends tonight.   我今晚會跟一群朋友出去。

(5) We just ate a bunch of grapes.   我們剛吃了一堆葡萄。

10 top of 在…之上

to**p** of ➡ tabav ['tɑbəv]

[p] 被兩個母音包圍，為了能使講話速度更自然、更快，[p] 會被稍稍強化成有聲的 [b]。

🌸 *Speak up*

(1) I think I left my keys on top of the coffee table.

我想我把鑰匙留在茶几上了。

(2) My favorite CD is always on top of the pile.

我總會把最喜愛的CD擺在最上層。

(3) It's only the top of the first inning.

現在才一局上半而已。

(4) I'm at the top of my class!

我是班上的資優生！

(5) I want a cherry on top of my ice cream.

我的冰淇淋上要加櫻桃。

I WANT A CHERRY ON TOP OF MY ICE CREAM.

30 can 與 can't
大不同 (1)

🔊 033

can
[kən]

● 助動詞 can 和 can't 雖然只有一字母之差，意思卻差很多，也是許多人聽力方面頭痛之處。can 當助動詞〔能夠〕時，母音 a[æ] 會弱化成 [ə]，只要輕輕發 [kən] 就可以了。

😊 *Speak up*

(1) I can do it on Sunday.   我星期天可以進行。

(2) No one can fix it.   沒人有辦法修理。

(3) He can eat a lot.   他食量很大。

(4) What can we do about it now?   我們現在該怎麼辦？

(5) Take your time. You can do it.   慢慢來，你一定可以辦到的。

(6) Where can we buy fresh shrimp?   哪裡可以買到新鮮的蝦子？

31 can 與 can't
大不同(2)

🔊 034

can't
[kæn]

● 發 can't 時，因為要強調不行/不能，不像 can [kən] 一樣隨隨便便就帶過了事。雖然 can't 會扎扎實實地把蝴蝶音 [æ] 發出來，但在大部分情況下，[t] 音會省略，所以唸成 [kæn]。

🌸 *Speak up*

(1) I can't promise you that.　　我不能跟你保證。

(2) I'm sorry, I can't come over on Sunday.　　很抱歉，我星期天沒辦法過去。

(3) Can't you tell him you're busy now?　　你難道不能跟他說你現在很忙嗎？

(4) I can't fix my bike by myself.　　我自己一個人沒辦法把腳踏車修好。

(5) I can't see anything with these glasses.　　戴這副眼鏡我根本什麼都看不到。

(6) If you can't beat them, join them.　　如果打不倒對手，就加入他們的陣營吧！(識時務者為俊傑)

能與不能之間的差異 - 〔can〕與〔can't〕聽力大考驗

1. I ___ do it!/ I ____ do it.

2. I ____ help you. / I ____ help you.

3. I ____ speak English. / I ____ speak English.

4. I ____ drive. / I ____ drive.

5. I ____ play the guitar, but my sister ____.

6. If you ____ go, ____ I have your ticket?

Answer Keys

1. I can do it! / I can't do it.
   我能辦到 / 我做不到。

2. I can help you. / I can't help you.
   我能幫你 / 我不能幫你的忙。

3. I can't speak English. / I can speak English.
   我不會說英文 / 我會說英文。

4. I can drive. / I can't drive.
   我會開車 / 我不會開車。

5. I can't play the guitar, but my sister can.
   我不會彈吉他，但我姊會。

6. If you can't go, can I have your ticket?
   如果你不能去，那可以把票給我嗎？

32 can當名詞時 的發音重點

036

can
[kæn]

●can 若是當名詞〔罐頭、罐子〕時，句中重音會落在 can 的 a[æ] 上，所以 [æ] 會發比較誇張的蝴蝶音。

🌼 *Speak up*

(1) The can opener is broken!　　開罐器壞了！

(2) The cat is in the garbage can.　　貓咪跑到垃圾桶裡去了。

(3) Buy me a can of soda.　　幫我買罐汽水。

(4) Where is the garbage can?　　垃圾桶在哪裡？

(5) We recycle cans and bottles.　　我們有回收瓶罐。

繞口令大集合 -
〔助動詞can〕與〔名詞can〕聽力辨析

1. A can opener can open cans.

   開罐器是用來打開罐頭的。

2. Can you help me open this can, please?

   能幫我開一下罐頭嗎?

3. Can you empty the garbage can for me?

   你能幫我倒一下垃圾嗎?

4. We can try to open the can with a knife.

   我們可以設法用刀子打開這個罐子。

5. She can have a lot of fun with kids just working with empty cans.

   她用空罐子就能和小朋友玩得不亦樂乎。

6. Their antique cans can fetch a good price at the auction.

   他們的古董罐能在拍賣會上賣個好價錢。

7. A can of spinach a day can really improve your health.

   一天一罐菠菜的確可以讓你更健康。

33 er 結尾 的捲舌音

🔊 038

er
[ɚ]

● [ɚ] 發音的位置是介在注音的 [さ] 和 [ㄦ] 之間，是有點捲又不會太捲的音喔。

🌼 *Speak up*
....

(1) I want to become a teacher.　　我要當老師。

(2) His daughter is very beautiful.　他的女兒很美。

(3) I think he's a very good writer.　我覺得他是個很棒的作家。

(4) The waiter at this　　　　　　　這家餐廳的服務生很帥。
restaurant is handsome.

(5) I want to talk to your　　　　　我要跟你經理談談。
manager.

(6) Who is your favorite singer?　你最喜歡的歌手是誰？

34 同一單字當名詞和動詞時重音不同

🔊 039

● 一個單字若是〔名詞 noun〕和〔動詞 verb〕同形，通常當名詞時，重音會在第一音節；當動詞時，重音則落在第二音節。

 *Speak up*

(1) There is no desert in Europe. 歐洲大陸沒有沙漠的足跡。

(2) All of his friends have deserted him. 所有的朋友都離他而去了。

(3) UFO stands for "unidentified flying object". UFO指的是「不明飛行物體」的意思。

(4) I object! 我反對！

(5) That college reject is my neighbor. 那個被退學的學生是我鄰居。

(6) His application to college was rejected. 他沒通過大學入學申請。

(7) The conflict in the Mid-East seems to go on forever.

中東各國的衝突似乎是沒有停歇的一天。

(8) Our personalities conflict.

我們倆的個性水火不容。

(9) His conduct during class was horrible!

他在課堂上的行為真是糟透了！

(10) This is my first time to conduct a choir.

這是我第一次指揮合唱團。

040

CHAPTER 4 實況對話總複習（I）
Practice Speaking Challenge!

▼ **Betty is a boss of a company and James works at the office.**
Betty是公司的主管，James是公司員工。

Betty: Hey James? What _____ now? _____ you

help me?

James: Sure Betty. _____ for you?

Betty: _____ put some big plants _____

my desk?

James: Where are the plants? At the _____the

stairs?

Betty: No, they're at _____the stairs.

James: Why do you want plants _____ your desk?

Betty: I _____ move them by myself. I already_____.

James: But why do you want _____ plants

there?

Betty: _____ our co-workers are distracting me.

James: Really? I thought we all _____ well _____.

Betty: I _____ work when there's _____

people walking by.

James: Oh, what about me? Do I bother you too?

Betty: No, you're on _____ the list. Let's do it.

James: There. We moved all of the plants. I'm tired.

Betty: Nice job! Thanks James. You can take

_____ the day off.

James: No thanks. I have _____ work _____ my

desk.

Betty: Oh, I thought you _____ go home

early _____.

James: I did _____ minutes ago, but now I need to

sit down!

041

CHAPTER 4 實況對話總複習（2）

Practice Speaking Challenge: teacher, daughter, writer, waiter, manager, singer, desert, object, reject, conflict, conduct.

▼ THE FUTURE IS WAITING FOR YOU!
許你一個未來！

Do you or your_____ feel like a _____? Do you worry about your future too much? Did your hopes _____ you? Does your life _____ with your dreams? At GOOD FUTURE we can tell you your lucky future for only one thousand dollars! Maybe your son will be a famous _____! Maybe you will be the _____ of a big company! I am sure your _____ can become a famous _____! Come to our downtown location! We are trained palm _____ from the Sahara _____! We have been _____ readings since we were children! Our _____ is always professional and we can settle all of your family's _____ for a very low price! _____ _____! The future is waiting for you! If you don't like your future we will give you a refund! Your satisfaction is guaranteed! Please bring a few personal _____ when you come. Come now! We do not _____ anybody!

ANSWER KEYS (1)

Chapter 4 Practice Speaking Challenge!

▼ **Betty is a boss of a company and James works at the office.**

Betty是公司的主管，James在辦公室工作。

Betty: Hey James? What are you do<u>ing</u> now? <u>Can</u> you help me?

嘿，James? 你在做什麼？可以幫我一個忙嗎？

James: Sure Betty. What <u>can</u> I do for you?

好啊，Betty。 需要我幫什麼忙呢？

Betty: <u>Can</u> you help me put some big plants <u>in front of</u> my desk?

你可以幫我把一些大型盆栽搬到我的辦公桌前面嗎？

James: Where are the plants? At the <u>top of</u> the stairs?

盆栽在哪？ 在最上層的樓梯嗎？

Betty: No, they're at <u>the bottom of</u> the stairs.

不是耶，是在樓梯最底部。

James: Why do you want plants <u>in front of</u> your desk?

為什麼要把盆栽擺在你桌子前面呢？

Betty: I can't move them by myself. I already tried <u>today</u>.

我自己搬不動。我今天已經試過了。

78

James: But why do you want a bunch of plants there?

但你為什麼要放一堆盆栽在你桌子前面呢？

Betty: Some of our co-workers are distracting me.

有些同事使我在工作時沒辦法集中精神。

James: Really? I thought we all worked well together.

真的嗎？我還以為我們大家一起工作得很融洽。

Betty: I can't work when there's a lot of people walking by.

當一堆人在我面前來來回回走動時，我就容易分心。

James: Oh, what about me? Do I bother you too?

呃，那我呢？我也影響到你了嗎？

Betty: No, you're on the bottom of the list. Let's do it.

沒有啦，你只擠得上黑名單的最底部而已。我們一起搬盆栽吧！

James: There. We moved all of the plants. I'm tired.

好了，終於搬完了，真累。

Betty: Nice job! Thanks James. You can take the rest of the day off.

太好了！真是謝謝你，James。你現在可以下班了。

James: No thanks. I have a lot of work on top of my desk.

不行！我桌上還堆了很多工作要做。

Betty: Oh, I thought you <u>wanted</u> to go home early <u>today</u>.

呃，我以為你想早點回家。

James: I did <u>a couple of</u> minutes ago, but now I need

to sit down!

幾分鐘前我的確有這樣的想法，但現在我只想先坐

下來再說！

Answer Keys (2)

Practice Speaking Challenge: teacher,
daughter, writer, waiter, manager,
singer, desert, object, reject, conflict, conduct.

▼ THE FUTURE IS WAITING FOR YOU!
許你一個未來！

Do you or your <u>son</u> or <u>daughter</u> feel like a <u>reject</u>? Do you worry about your future too much? Did your hopes <u>desert</u> you? Does your life <u>conflict</u> with your dreams? At GOOD FUTURE we can tell you your lucky future for only one thousand dollars! Maybe your son will be a famous <u>singer</u>! Maybe you will be the <u>manager</u> of a big company! I am sure your <u>daughter</u> can become a famous <u>writer</u>! Come to our downtown location! We are trained palm readers from the Sahara desert! We have been conducting readings since we were children! Our conduct is always professional and we can settle all of your family's conflicts for a very low price! Don't object! The future is waiting for you! If you don't like your future we will give you a refund! Your satisfaction is guaranteed! Please bring a few personal objects when you come. Come now! We do not reject anybody!

你或是你兒子女兒是否總是諸事不順？你是否很擔心未來？你的希望是否早已成為幻影？你的生活是否和夢想背道而馳？來「GOOD FUTURE」，只要1000元，我們便能為你找到屬於未來的幸運！或許你兒子會是個赫赫有名的歌手！或許你會成為一家大公司的高級主管！我敢保證你的女兒一定會成為叱吒文壇的作家！趕快來我們位於市區的服務據點！我們是一群來自薩哈拉沙漠，且受過專業訓練的手相算命師！我們從很小的時候就開始幫人看手相！透過我們專業的指引，只要很低的價錢，就能幫你排解家庭糾紛！未來正等著你，請不要拒絕它！若你不喜歡我們為你創造的未來，我們一律退費！當你過來時，請帶幾樣私人的物品！現在就馬上行動！我們很樂意為每個人服務，來者不拒！

CHAPTER 5

基本連音要訣

當〔子音碰到子音〕或是〔子音碰到母音〕時，會形成不等的消音或是變音。

35 相同子音相遇
只要唸一次

◀》042

What a stupid donkey.

Nice skirt!

I won't tell.

● 當兩個相同的子音湊在一起時，只要唸一次就行了。

s-s, t-t, d-d, p-p, k-k, g-g, f-f, v-v…依此類推。

Speak up

(1) Stop poking me!	別再煩我了！
(2) What time is it, Tom?	Tom，現在幾點了？
(3) It's so hot today.	今天真是有夠熱。
(4) I ate fried dumplings.	我吃了鍋貼。
(5) That girl likes you.	那個女生喜歡你。
(6) Steve vacuumed the room.	Steve用吸塵器打掃了房間。
(7) That cook can't cook.	這個廚師的廚藝糟透了。

36 不同子音相遇
第一個被消滅
（弱化或消音）

◄))043

Help me!
(因為緊跟在後的子音 [m] 的關係，所以 [p] 弱化)

Sit down.
(因 [t] 和 [d] 發音位置相近，所以 [t] 消音)

Don't worry.
(因 [w] 的關係，所以 [t] 消音)

I like Bob.
(因為緊跟在後的子音 [b] 的關係，所以 [k] 弱化)

Would you mind my sitting here?
(因為緊跟在後的子音 [m] 的關係，所以 [d] 消音)

It's a big ball.
(因為緊跟在後的子音 [b] 的關係，所以 [g] 弱化)

Let me go.

(因為緊跟在後的子音 [m] 的關係，所以 [t] 消音)

Give me.

(因為緊跟在後的子音 [m] 的關係，所以 [v] 消音)

● 句子中相鄰的兩個單字，若前一個單字的結尾是子音，而後一個單字也是以子音開頭的話，當兩個相遇的子音剛好發音位置又特別相近，或是後面的子音特別強勢時，通常前一個單字的子音會有弱化的現象，也就是說該子音會被輕輕地帶過，說話速度一快，甚至會有消音的現象。

Speak up

(1) Can you give me a hand? 　　能幫我個忙嗎？

(2) What would you like to eat? 　你想吃什麼？

(3) Would you mind watching my bag? 　你可以幫我看一下包包嗎？

(4) That was fun! 　　真好玩！

(5) The ground looks wet. 　地板看起來溼溼的。

(6) Don't worry about it. 　別擔心。

(7) Wow! This is a really big party! 　哇！這個派對排場真大！

(8) Help me! I can't swim! 　救命啊！我不會游泳！

(9) My cat didn't come home last night. 　我的貓昨天晚上沒回家。

(10) I sold my books to the bookstore. 　我把書賣給了書店。

37 無聲子音變有聲

[p]→[b]・[t]→[d]
[k]→[g]・[s]→[z]

🔊 044

wee**k**end ['wigɛnd]

I promise to visit you on the weekend.

我週末一定會去看你。

fes**t**ival ['fɛsdəvḷ]

We met a lot of people at the music festival.

我們在音樂節上認識好多人。

se**c**ond ['sɛgənd]

Wait a second.

等一下。

● 當無聲子音 [p][t][k][s] 不在重音節時，會被緊跟在後的母音強化，變成有聲子音 [b][d][g][z]。

🌸 *Speak up*

....

(1) Please whisper, sir. This is a library.

先生，請保持輕聲細語。這裡是圖書館。

(2) What are you cooking? It smells great!

你在煮什麼？好香喔！

(3) He doesn't deserve to win. He cheated!

他沒資格贏，因為他作弊。

(4) We stayed at a five-star resort hotel.

我們待在五星級的度假飯店。

(5) Sorry, we're closing up in five minutes.

很抱歉，我們再五分鐘就打烊了。

(6) I forget. Is today Saturday, or Sunday?

我忘了，今天是星期六還是星期日？

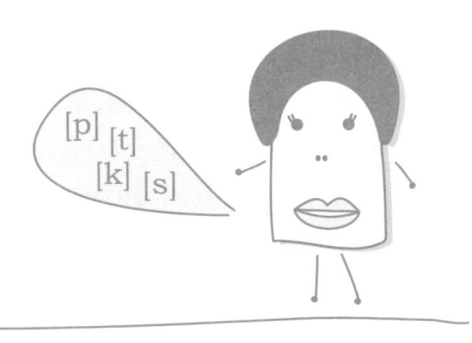

38 摩擦音[s][f] 的魔法

🔊 045

skirt [sgɜt]　　**sp**eed [sbid]

staff [sdæf]　　lef**t**over ['lefd͵ovə]

● 當無聲的摩擦音 [s] 或 [f]，碰上無聲的塞音 [k]、[p]、[t] 時，會產生強化作用，使 [k]、[p]、[t] 變成有聲版本的 [g]、[b]、[d]。如 skirt 的 k [k]，因受摩擦音 [s] 的影響，會發成有聲的 [g]。

🐑 *Speak up*

(1) The skirt is too short for you.　這件裙子你穿太短了。

(2) Do you have any skills?　你有任何技能嗎？

(3) Please speak slowly.　請說慢點。

(4) Do you believe in spirits?　你相信有靈魂的存在嗎？

(5) Don't stir the noodles.　別翻攪麵條。

(6) Who are you staring at?　你在瞪誰？

(7) I hate lifting heavy boxes.　我討厭抬笨重的箱子。

(8) Do you believe in an afterlife?　你相信有來生嗎？

(9) I like to sleep in the afternoon.　我喜歡在下午睡個午覺。

子音母音連著唸

🔊 046

hold on
['hold͜ɑn]

● 在句子中，若子音結尾的單字與母音開頭的單字相遇，子音和母音就會形成連音，快快唸過去囉！

🌸 *Speak up*

....

(1) I'm trying to save up some money.　　我正努力存一點錢。

(2) She saved up her money for a year.　　她存了一年的錢。

(3) The baby cried all the way home.　　小baby一路哭回家。

(4) Please don't shout at me.　　請不要對我大吼大叫。

(5) Wake up! You're late for work!　　起床！你上班遲到了！

(6) Why does he always doze off in class？　　為什麼他上課老是打瞌睡？

(7) There's a lemon on the table.　　桌上有顆檸檬。

CHAPTER 5 實況對話總複習
Practice Speaking Challenge!

▼ **Harry and Susan are on the train. Harry asks Susan for directions.**
Harry和Susan在同班火車上，Harry向Susan問路。

Harry: Sorry to bother you. Would you mind telling me where the beach is?

不好意思，打擾一下。你可以告訴我海邊怎麼去嗎？

Susan: Sure. Give me a second. I have a lot of maps in my bag.

當然。等我一下，我包包裡有很多地圖。

Harry: Oh, you have very many maps. Can you find the beach?

喔，你地圖真的很多耶。你知道海邊在哪個位置嗎？

Susan: Yes, the beach is just ten minutes from the next train station.

知道啊，海邊就在離下個車站十分鐘的路程。

Harry: Thank you. It's nice of you to help people who are lost.

謝謝。你真是個大好人，能對我們這些迷路的人伸出援手。

Susan: No problem my friend. Why are you going to the beach?

不用客氣啦。 你為什麼要去海邊呢？

Harry: I'm going surfing. I will surf for a few hours.

我要去衝浪。我打算在海邊衝個幾小時的浪。

Susan: That sounds so fun! Have you mastered it yet?

聽起來好像很好玩！你是衝浪專家囉？

Harry: No. I'm becoming good at it, but the sea is my master! Can you surf?

不是啦！不過我的衝浪技術越來越成熟了，但人再怎麼厲害還是敵不過大海的！你玩衝浪嗎？

Susan: No. I'm not skilled at sports. Anyway, after work I'm too tired.

我不會衝浪。我運動完全不行。每天下班後都累死了。

Harry: Where do you work?

你在什麼公司工作？

Susan: I work at a map publishing company. I make cardboard maps.

我在一家地圖出版社工作。我專門製作紙板地圖。

Harry: You are skilled too!

你也有專精的地方啊！

Susan: Yes, I could describe many places on a map!

我可以在地圖上指出很多地方！

Harry: I guess so. This stop is mine. See you later! Thanks again!

我想也是。我要下車了。再見囉！非常感謝！

Susan: Wait up! I want to come with you…

等等！我想跟你去…

Harry: But what about your really nice job?

但你這份優渥的工作怎麼辦？

Susan: I always look at maps. Let me go to a real place today.

我一直活在地圖的世界裡，今天就讓我去體認一下真實的世界吧。

伶牙俐齒－特殊消音與變音

在美式口語發音中，有些音會消失或變音，比如〔center會唸成cener〕、〔listen會唸成lisen〕、〔winter會唸成winer〕、〔sweater會唸成sweader〕，這些神奇的變化在本章中有詳盡的說明。

．．．．．．．．．．．．．．．．．．．．．．．．．．．．．．．．．．．．．．

註 本章與第7章所出現的藍色字，如cener (P93)、canai (P115)，是表示口語發音的唸法，並非一般寫法。

 **40** 字中[n]前[t]後
[t]被消滅

<audio>048</audio>

cen~~t~~er → **cener** [ˈsɛnə˞]
win~~t~~er → **winer** [ˈwɪnə˞]

● 單字中，[n] 在前 [t] 在後 — [t] 的特殊消音：在單字中，若 [t] 不在重音節，而且前面又遇到天敵 [n] 時，[t] 就會被消滅。[t] 的消失是因為 [n][t] 兩個音發音位置實在太相近，而 [t] 又是無聲子音，為使說話速度更快，只好捨棄 [t] 囉！

Speak up

(1) How was your winter vacation? | 你寒假過得怎樣？

(2) I think she dropped your computer accidentally. | 我覺得她是不小心摔到電腦的。

(3) Excuse me, where is the city center? | 請問一下，市中心在哪裡？

(4) In Toronto we saw the C.N. Tower. | 我們在多倫多參觀了西恩塔。

(5) A large percentage of people believe in UFOs. | 很多人相信幽浮的存在。

(6) Please enter your username and password. | 請輸入你的帳號和密碼。

(7) The printer is making strange noises. | 這台印表機發出奇怪的聲音。

 **字中[t]前[n]後 [t]半消音**

impor~t~ant → **impor_ant**
[ɪmˈpɔr_n̩t]

forgo~tt~en → **forga_en**
[fɚˈgɑ_n̩]

cer~t~ain → **cer_ain**
[ˈsɝ_n̩]

● 單字中，[t] 在前 [n] 在後— [t] 的半消音：這裡還是因為 t,n 發音位置很接近，所以 [t] 音只輕輕帶過，甚至消音，停一拍，最後以 [n̩] 結束。這個音有點難度，請務必跟著MP3多練幾遍！

🌸 *Speak up*
....

(1) Health is very important.　　健康很重要。

94

(2) Can you give me a cotton bud? 可以給我一支棉花棒嗎？

(3) She hasn't written a letter to me in a while. 她已經有一陣子沒寫信給我了。

(4) Have you forgotten everything I said? 你是不是已經忘了我說的每一件事？

(5) My parents live in Manhattan. 我爸媽住在曼哈頓。

(6) The button on my shirt fell off. 我襯衫的鈕扣掉了。

(7) I think I passed the test, but I'm not certain. 我猜我考試有過，但不是很確定。

(8) I was bitten by my own dog! 我被自己的狗咬了一口！

(9) My new kittens sleep in my shoes. 我的一窩新小貓睡在我的鞋子裡。

(10) Have you ever climbed a mountain? 你爬過山嗎？

(11) Don't forget your mittens. It's cold outside! 別忘了帶手套，外面很冷！

字中 [s] 前 [t] 後 [t] 被消滅

🔊 050

listen → lisen ['lɪsn̩]

● 單字中，[s] 在前 [t] 在後──[t] 的消音：[s][t] 兩個音都是無聲子音，兩個一起唸時，實在蠻吃力的，當[t]不在重音位置時，就會偷偷被省略掉囉！

🌼 *Speak up*

....

ⓐ [t]在字中的消音 (1)

(1) Listen up, I have to tell you something.　聽好！我有話要跟你說。

(2) Please fasten your seatbelt.　請繫上安全帶。

ⓑ [t]在字中的消音 (2)

(1) I had visited a castle last summer.　我去年夏天參觀了一座城堡。

(2) The boy is blowing a whistle.　這個男孩在吹口哨。

(3) This shopping mall is bustling!　這家購物中心人潮真多！

(4) Can you hear the leaves rustling?　你有聽到樹葉搖曳的沙沙聲嗎？

(5) The shop owner tried to hustle me!　這家店的老闆千方百計想推銷我東西！

43 尾音[t]後接子音 [t]被消滅

■))051

trust me → **trasme** [ˈtrʌsmi]

● 若 [t] 後面接的是子音的話，[t] 自然而然會被省略：相反地，若 [t] 後面接的是母音的話，[t] 則不會被刪掉，而會形成子母連音。

🌸 *Speak up*

(1) The dust makes my nose itchy. 　　灰塵讓我鼻子很癢。

(2) Did you watch the weather forecast for tomorrow? 　　你有看明天的氣象報告嗎？

(3) Do you trust me or not? 　　你相不相信我？

(4) I almost dropped the food! 　　食物差點被我摔在地上！

(5) The past can't be changed. 　　過去的事是不能改變的。

(6) She has a really fast scooter. 　　她有一台跑得很快的機車。

(7) I bought this coat for one hundred dollars. 　　我花了一百元買了這件外套。

(8) Your rent was due ten days ago. 　　你房租十天前就到期了。

(9) Please wait for me, I'm coming! 　　請等我一下，我馬上來！

44 尾音[t]後接母音兩者連音

hot outside → **hadousaid**
['hɑdausaɪd]

● [t] 遇母音的連音：若 [t] 後面接母音，[t]不會被刪掉，而會形成子母連音；也因為 [t] 和母音連音，造成[t] 的強化，而變成有聲的 [d]。

🌸 *Speak up*

(1) The hot spring is west of here. 　從這邊往西走，你就會看到溫泉了。

(2) There's a ghost under my bed! 　有鬼在我床底下！

(3) I put the shopping list in my pocket. 　我把購物清單放在口袋。

(4) It's too hot outside to play tennis. 　現在外面太熱了，不適合打網球。

(5) He ate the hot pot all by himself! 　他一個人把火鍋全吃光了！

(6) Help! There's a rat on the porch! 　救命呀！走廊有一隻老鼠！

(7) That blue boat is full of lobsters. 　那條藍色的船上滿載著龍蝦。

(8) Please visit us again soon. 　歡迎下次再光臨。

[t][d] 接 **-ly** 的消音

🔊 053

mos~~t~~ly → **mosly** ['moslɪ]

●[t] 遇 -ly 的消音：為了使發音能更順暢，[t] 音在這裡理所當然被消音了；而 [d] 為 [t] 的有聲版本，所以兩者遇到 ly 時都會沒輒，淪為被消音的下場。

😊 *Speak up*

. . . .

(1) Recently I've been practicing golf.　最近我在練高爾夫球。

(2) The society here is changing rapidly.　社會變遷得很快速。

(3) He talks differently when he drinks.　他喝醉酒時會語無倫次。

(4) These new laptops are very costly.　新款的筆記型電腦很貴。

(5) This store sells mostly computers.　這家店賣的大部分是電腦產品。

(6) The jazz band played perfectly!　這個爵士樂團演奏得很棒。

(7) Honestly, I like living in the city.　坦白說，我喜歡住在城市。

[h]什麼情況
會消音？

bea̶t̶ h̶im → **bidim** [ˈbidɪm]

● h 的消音：為使發音速度更快，這些不像動詞、名詞有實質意義的字，通常開頭的 h 就會被消音囉！

> **以下所列的字，h 不發音**
>
> h̶ave・h̶as・h̶e・h̶im・h̶is・h̶er・h̶ers・wh̶at・
> wh̶o・wh̶ere・wh̶en・wh̶ich

😊 *Speak up*

(1) I love h̶er.　　　　　　　　　　我愛她。

(2) Beat h̶im up.　　　　　　　　　海扁他一頓。

(3) I don't know wh̶o did it.　　　　我不知道是誰幹的好事。

(4) Do you remember h̶is name?　你還記得他的名字嗎？

(5) Where h̶ave you been?　　　　你到哪裡去了？

(6) I know wh̶at you mean.　　　　我懂你的意思。

(7) Ask h̶im where he's from.　　　問他是哪裡人。

(8) Tell me wh̶ich song you prefer.　告訴我你喜歡哪首歌。

(9) I was sleeping wh̶en you
　　called.　　　　　　　　　　　你打來的時候我在睡覺。

47 助動詞+have
的連音變化

🔊 055

could h̸av̸e → could'a
['kudə]

● **助動詞 + have 大變身**：一些固定與 have 一搭一唱的組合，會因為 have [h] 的消音，而跟 have 產生連音變化。請記住，could have 的縮寫 could've 不唸 [kuv]，而是唸 [kudəv]，[v] 的音只要門牙碰一下嘴唇一秒即可，不用使力地發出來，於是有些懶人把 could've 改寫成 could'a，其他組合以此類推。

---

have 的超級組合：

could h̸ave → could'v̸e → could'a ['kudə]

should h̸ave → should'v̸e → should'a ['ʃudə]

would h̸ave → would'v̸e → would'a ['wudə]

mus̸t h̸ave → mus̸t'v̸e → mus̸t'a ['mʌsdə]

migh̸t h̸ave → migh̸t'v̸e → migh̸t'a ['maɪdə]

wha̸t h̸ave → wha̸t'v̸e → wha̸t'a ['wɑdə]

✿ *Speak up*

....

(1) You could'a come here earlier.　　　你應該可以早點來的。

(2) You really should'a told me earlier.　　　你該早點告訴我的。

(3) You could'a called me yesterday.　　　你昨天可以打電話給我的。

(4) I would'a gone, but I was sick.　　　我本來要去的，但我生病了所以沒去。

(5) It's cold. I must'a left the window open.　　　好冷，一定是窗戶還開著。

(6) They might'a gone home already.　　　他們應該早就回家了。

(7) What'a you been doing recently?　　　你最近在忙什麼？

WHAT'A YOU BEEN DOING RECENTLY?

48 [t] 夾在兩個母音中間時怎麼唸？

■》056

sweater → sweader
['swɛdə]

● [t] 的變音・[t]→[彈舌音d]：當無聲的 [t] 夾在兩個母音中間時，會被母音強化，而變成[彈舌音d]；[彈舌音d]到底和普通 [d] 有什麼不同？[彈舌音d]比普通的 [d] 要來得柔一些，發音的速度也會比較快。

🌸 *Speak up*

ⓐ 單字裡面的〔彈舌音d〕

(1) San Francisco is a beautiful city. 　　舊金山是座美麗的城市。

(2) She's a very pretty girl. 　　她是個很漂亮的女孩。

(3) This romance movie is pitiful. 　　這部愛情電影很賺人熱淚。

(4) I'll clean up my room on Saturday. 　　我星期六會把房間打掃乾淨。

(5) Don't forget to water the flowers. 　　別忘了澆花。

(6) The sweater suits you well. 　　這件毛衣很適合你。

b 句子裡面的〔彈舌音d〕

(1) Shut up！   閉嘴！

(2) Put it in the oven for ten   把它放到烤箱十分鐘。
    minutes.

(3) You can sit in the back seat.   你可以坐在後排的位置。

(4) What a pity!   真可惜！

(5) Let's meet at eight o'clock.   我們就八點見吧。

(6) Don't forget about our   別忘了我們還有會要開。
    meeting.

49

-tter
的習慣唸法

■))057

li**tt**er → **lidder** [ˈlɪdɚ]

● -tter 也瘋狂・**tt**er[tɚ] → [dɚ]：記得我們之前有討論到無聲子音[p][t][k]若在輕音節，會被後面的母音強化成有聲的[b][d][g]嗎？（請參考第37條要訣）-tter的變化也是相同道理，就是[t]會變成[彈舌音d]，-tter唸成[dɚ]。由於 -tter 的單字實在是太多，用到的機會很多，所以在這裡特別獨立出來練習。

🌸 *Speak up*

(1) Pass me the bu**tt**er please. 請把奶油給我。

(2) The bu**tt**erfly is flu**tt**ering its wings. 蝴蝶拍動著翅膀。

(3) No li**tt**ering. 請勿亂丟垃圾。

(4) Did you get my le**tt**er? 你有收到我的信嗎？

(5) She is my son's new babysi**tt**er. 她是我兒子的新褓母。

(6) Recently your cat looks fa**tt**er. 你的貓最近看起來變胖了。

(7) I'm fla**tt**ered by what you said. 你的話真是讓我受寵若驚。

(8) Don't worry, it doesn't ma**tt**er. 別擔心，沒關係的。

50 -ttle 的習慣唸法

🔊 058

little → liddle ['lɪd!]

● [t]遇到l也有同樣遭遇，[t]變為微弱的[彈舌音d]，然後很快和[!]結合，所以整個字的發音重點是放在[!]上。發此音時舌頭要動得很快，請務必跟著MP3多練幾遍！

🌼 *Speak up*

. . . .

(1) I'm a little upset.   我有一點生氣。

(2) He died in a battle.   他在戰役中身亡。

(3) Can I have a bottle of water?   可以給我一瓶水嗎？

(4) Have you ever seen a rattlesnake?   你有見過響尾蛇嗎？

(5) My father owns a hundred cattle.(cattle已經是複數了，不需加s)   我爸爸養了一百頭牛。

(6) This shuttlebus goes downtown.   這輛接駁車是開往市區的。

(7) Grandma's bones are brittle.   奶奶的骨頭很脆弱。

-sk, -st
後接 S 怎麼唸？

masks

🔊059

tests

● -sk, -st 後面接 s 是很難唸的音。 sks, sts 兩個音唸起來就像 s+注音的ㄎ。

🌸 *Speak up*

. . . .

(1) Let's wear masks to the party!　我們戴面具去參加派對吧！

(2) I have two tests today.　我今天有兩個考試。

(3) My son always asks for money.　我兒子老是跟我要錢。

(4) We share the household tasks.　我們一起分擔家務。

(5) Where are the computer disks?　電腦磁片在哪裡？

(6) He still believes that Santa exists.　他相信聖誕老人的存在。

(7) She says she can see ghosts!　她說她看得到鬼！

(8) Taiwan has many great artists.　台灣有很多很棒的藝術家。

(9) The tourists asked for directions.　旅客問路。

107

52 -th後接s th消音

🔊 060

mon~~th~~s [mʌnz]

● -th 後面緊跟著 [s] 很難發音，所以 th 會消音，而後面的 s 發成有聲的 [z]。

🌸 *Speak up*

(1) I gave my old clothes to a charity.　　　我把舊衣捐給慈善機構。

(2) She had a baby only two months ago.　　　她二個月前才生了baby。

(3) I like to take hot baths in summer.　　　我夏天喜歡泡熱水澡。

(4) Are there bicycle paths near here?　　　這裡有自行車專用道嗎？

(5) The telephone booths are upstairs.　　　電話亭在樓上。

(6) My teacher taught me many truths.　　　我的老師教我很多真理。

061

CHAPTER 6 實況對話總複習
Practice Speaking Challenge!

▼ **Colleagues Richard and Jennifer have returned from vacation.**
Richard 和 Jennifer 分別度完假返回工作崗位。

Jennifer: Welcome back Richard. Did you _____ on vacation?

Richard: _____. I'm still _____ and dancing to island music.

Jennifer: _____ island?! _____? You look _____.

Richard: I feel _____. I took a trip to Hawaii. _____!

Jennifer: Really? I _____ to Hawaii was too _____.

Richard: It _____ a lot to fly there, _____ the sights are free!

Jennifer: _____ did you do there? Did you go _____?

Richard: No. I like to _____, so I visited _____ volcanoes.

Jennifer: _____!? You _____ accidentally fallen in!

Richard: _____, it was safe. Anyway, _____

_____!

Jennifer: I _____, but there are _____ in

funny _____!

Richard: Hee hee! And _____! _____ go for

vacation?

Jennifer: _____! I took an _____

to France!

Richard: Oh! How was the weather? _____

said _____ hot.

Jennifer: _____ warm. _____

___ than Hawaii.

Richard: _____ France! You _____ me a

_____!

Jennifer: _____, and _____

_____.

Richard: Great! What did you buy? _____?

_____? _____?

Jennifer: I _____ about you. I _____

of wine!

Richard: _____ a lot. I only _____

___ for you.

Jennifer: What?! That's _____?! Give me back

the wine!

Answer Keys
Chapter 6 Practice Speaking Challenge!

▼ **Colleagues Richard and Jennifer have returned from vacation.**
Richard 和 Jennifer 分別度完假返回工作崗位。

Jennifer: Welcome back Richard. Did you get enough rest on vacation?

歡迎歸國，Richard，在假期中休息夠了吧？

Richard: Not at all. I'm still listening and dancing to island music.

還沒勒，我還沉醉在島國音樂中。

Jennifer: Which island?! Where did you go? You look a little better.

哪個島？你去哪裡度假？你看起來有精神多了。

Richard: I feel better. I took a trip to Hawaii. It went perfectly!

我覺得心情好多了。我去了夏威夷一趟，很棒的一次旅程！

Jennifer: Really? I thought a vacation to Hawaii was too costly.

真的嗎？ 去夏威夷度假不是很貴嗎？

Richard: It costs a lot to fly there, but the sights are free!

坐一趟飛機去那裡是要花很多錢沒錯，但美景可是免費的！

Jennifer: What did you do there? Did you go water-skiing?

你在那裡做了什麼？你有去滑水嗎？

Richard: No. I like to take risks, so I visited a lot of volcanoes.

沒有。我愛冒險，所以我去參觀了很多火山。

Jennifer: What!? You could'a accidentally fallen in!

什麼！？你不小心會跌下去的！

Richard: Trust me, it was safe. Anyway, you should'a come!

相信我，安啦。你應該來的！

Jennifer: I would'a, but there are mostly tourists in funny clothes!

我是應該去沒錯，但你到處可看到旅客穿著滑稽的衣服走來走去。

Richard: Hee hee! And masks! Where did you go for vacation?

嘻嘻！還有面具！你去哪裡度假了？

Jennifer: Fasten your seatbelt! I took an international flight to France!

「繫好您的安全帶」，我飛往法國度假！

Richard: Oh! How was the weather? The forecast said it was hot.

喔！那裡的天氣如何？ 氣象報告說那裡很熱。

Jennifer: It was a little warm. It might'a been hotter than Hawaii.

是有點熱，應該是比夏威夷熱吧。

Richard: Tell me about France! You should'a written me a letter!

跟我說說你的法國之旅吧！你應該寫封信給我才對！

Jennifer: The cities are bustling, and the mountain castles are pretty.

法國的城市人潮很擁擠，但坐落在山間的城堡很美。

Richard: Great! What did you buy? A button? Clothes? Mittens?

真棒！那你買了什麼？ 鈕扣？衣服？手套？

Jennifer: I haven't forgotten about you. I got you a bottle of wine!

我可沒忘了你的份。我買了一瓶酒要給你！

Richard: That must'a cost a lot. I only got butter cookies for you.

應該很貴吧！我只買了奶油餅乾給你。

Jennifer: What?! That's all you have?! Give me back the wine!

什麼！？ 你就給我這個！？把酒還我！

CHAPTER 7

高頻率連音組合

以下都是很常聽到的連音組合，多多練習你就能克服聽力盲點，並說出一口好英語喔。

53 can I
的連音變化

■)) 062

can I → canai
[kənaɪ]

🌼 *Speak up*

(1) Can I ask you a question?   我能問你一個問題嗎？
(2) Where can I go?   我能去哪裡？
(3) What can I do?   我能怎麼辦？
(4) Who can I talk to?   我能跟誰談？
(5) When can I leave?   我什麼時候可以走？

54 could I
的連音變化

◀)063

could I → cudai
[kudaɪ]

😊 *Speak up*

(1) Could I please have this dance? 　　能有這個榮幸和你跳支舞嗎？

(2) How could I be so blind? 　　我怎麼會這麼盲目呢？

(3) Could I speak to you for a minute? 　　能跟你借幾分鐘說話嗎？

(4) Could I offer you a drink? 　　我能請你喝飲料嗎？

(5) What could I have done wrong? 　　我到底是哪裡做錯了？

55 what can I
的連音變化

🔊064

wha͡t can I
→ wacanai
[wɑkənaɪ]

🌸 *Speak up*

(1) What can I do to make you happy?   怎麼做才能使你快樂呢？

(2) What can I cook for you?   你要我煮什麼給你吃？

(3) What can I get you?   你想要什麼？

(4) What can I do for you?   有什麼我能為你效勞之處嗎？

(5) What can I help you with?   有什麼我可以幫忙的嗎？

56 what is it
的連音變化

🔊 065

what is it → waizi
[wɑɪzɪ]

🌸 *Speak up*

(1) What is it like outside? 　　外面的情況如何？

(2) What is it used for? 　　這東西是做什麼用的？

(3) What is it going to cost? 　　這個東西要花多少錢？

(4) What is it that makes you 　　她到底哪一點值得讓你為她
crazy about her? 　　神魂顛倒？

(5) What is it made of? 　　這東西是什麼做的？

57 what do you
的連音變化

🔊 066

what do you

→ **wadaya**

[wɑdəjə]

● What do you 在 [h]、[t] 消音、do you 弱化後，實際的發音變成了 wadaya。

🌸 *Speak up*

....

(1) What do you like on your pizza?   你披薩要加什麼料？

(2) What do you think of her?   你覺得她如何？

(3) What do you like to watch on TV?   你喜歡看什麼電視節目？

(4) What do you think you're doing?   你在搞什麼名堂？

(5) What do you want to eat for dinner?   你晚餐想吃什麼？

is she
的連音變化

🔊 067

i~~s~~ she → **ishi**
[ɪʃi]

🌸 *Speak up*

....

(1) Is she pretty? 她漂亮嗎？

(2) Is she here? 她在這裡嗎？

(3) Is she around? 她在附近嗎？

(4) Is she your girlfriend? 她是你女朋友嗎？

(5) Is she busy tomorrow? 她明天忙嗎？

59 is he
的連音變化

🔊 068

is he ➜ izi
[ɪzi]

🌸 *Speak up*

(1) Is he at home? 　　　　　　　　　他在家嗎？

(2) Is he joining us for dinner? 　　他有要和我們一起吃晚餐嗎？

(3) Is he going to quit smoking? 　他準備要戒菸嗎？

(4) Is he out with his 　　　　　　　他跟他的同事一起出去嗎？
    colleagues?

(5) Is he your landlord? 　　　　　　他是你的房東嗎？

60 is it
的連音變化

is it → **izi**

[ɪzɪ]

● is it 在連音變化後是不是和 is he 唸起來很像呢？ "is it" 和 "is he" 最大差別是， "is he" 在 h 消音後成為[ɪzi]，其尾音是長音的 [i]，而 "is it"[ɪzɪ] 的尾音則是短音的 [ɪ]。

Speak up

(1) Is it OK?   還可以嗎？

(2) Is it allowed to park here?   這裡能停車嗎？

(3) Is it Friday already?   已經星期五了嗎？

(4) Is it OK if I sit here?   我可以坐這裡嗎？

(5) Is it me, or is it hot in here?   是只有我覺得熱，還是這裡本來就很熱？

61 is that
的連音變化

🔊070

is ~~that~~ → **iza**
[ɪzæ]

😊 *Speak up*

....

(1) Is that what you want? 　那是你想要的嗎？
(2) Is that your car? 　那是你的車嗎？
(3) Is that going to be enough? 　那樣夠嗎？
(4) Is that what you told her? 　你是那樣跟她說的嗎？
(5) Is that what you meant? 　你是這個意思嗎？
(6) Is that a good idea? 　那樣好嗎？

62

it is
的連音變化

■))071

it is → idiz
[ɪdɪz]

● "it is" 的 t 因為夾在兩個母音中間，所以會稍稍強化成彈舌音 d。

🌸 Speak up

(1) That's how it is.　　　　　　　事情就是這樣。

(2) Do you know where it is?　　　你知道它在哪裡嗎？

(3) Here it is, I found it.　　　　　就在這裡，終於找到它了。

(4) I know who it is.　　　　　　　我知道是誰在搞鬼。

(5) Can you tell me where it is?　　可以告訴我它在哪裡嗎？

(6) Yes, it is.　　　　　　　　　　是的。

63 need a
的連音變化

🔊072

need a → **needa**
[nidə]

🌸 *Speak up*

(1) Do you need a car?   你需要車嗎？

(2) I need a new computer.   我需要一台新電腦。

(3) I need a vacation.   我需要度個假。

(4) Do you need a ride?   你需要搭便車嗎？

(5) I need a pen and a piece of   我需要紙跟筆。
     paper.

64 take it
的連音變化

🔊073

take it → **tegi**
[tegɪ]

● 無聲 k 因夾在兩個母音中間，所以強化成 g 音。it 的 t 被消音。

🌸 *Speak up*

(1) Take it easy on him.   饒了他吧。
(2) Don't take it as an insult.   別把它當成是一種侮辱。
(3) I can't take it anymore!   我再也無法忍受了！
(4) I take it as a responsibility.   我把它當作是一種責任。
(5) Take it easy.   放輕鬆。

have a
的連音變化

🔊 074

have a → ava
[ævə]

● 若 have 出現在句首時 (通常是問句或祈使句)，[h] 通常不會被消音，如祝別人旅途愉快 "Have a nice trip."，這裡的 have 會完整地唸出來；只有在句中受到其他單字影響時，[h] 才會被「滅口」。

🌸 *Speak up*

. . . .

(1) I have a girlfriend.   我有女朋友。

(2) You have a sweet home.   你有個甜蜜的家。

(3) We have a lot of DVDs.   我們有很多DVD。

(4) They have a cute dog!   他們有隻很可愛的狗！

(5) I have a secret to tell you.   我有個秘密要告訴你。

(6) I have a cold.   我感冒了。

66 use a 的連音變化

075

use a → uza

[juzə]

Speak up

(1) Use a spoon, please! 請使用湯匙！

(2) She'll use a computer more at her new job. 她的新工作會比較常使用電腦。

(3) Use a knife, it's easier. 用刀子會比較容易。

(4) You may use a pen or pencil. 你可以使用普通的筆或鉛筆。

(5) Do you use a lot of make-up? 你有用很多化妝品嗎？

(6) May I use a pencil? 我可以用鉛筆嗎？

67 give me 的連音變化

gi~ve me → gimme [gɪmi]

● 因為 [v] 和 [m] 都是子音的關係，所以 [v] 被消音。有時也會看到 gimme 這種強調口語的寫法。

🌸 *Speak up*

(1) Give me a break, will you?　　別煩我，好嗎？
Gimme a break, will you?

(2) What are you gonna give me　你耶誕節要送我什麼禮物？
for Christmas?
What are you gonna gimme
for Christmas?

(3) Give me a hand, please.　　請幫幫我吧！
Gimme a hand, please.

(4) Give me a reason not to　給我一個不該討厭你的理由。
hate you.
Gimme a reason not to hate
you.

(5) Give me a few more minutes.　給我幾分鐘的時間。
Gimme a few more minutes.

(6) Don't give me excuses.　別找藉口。
Don't gimme excuses.

68 let me
的連音變化

🔊 077

let me → lemme
[lɛmi]

● 在 let me 中，因為 [t] 和 [m] 都是子音，所以 [t] 被消音了。（請參考第 36 條要訣）你有時也會在強調口語的書寫中看到 lemme 這種寫法。

😊 *Speak up*

. . . .

(1) Let me find out for you.　　　　　我幫你找找。
　　Lemme find out for you.

(2) Let me guess.　　　　　　　　　　讓我猜一下。
　　Lemme guess.

(3) Let me try.　　　　　　　　　　　讓我試試。
　　Lemme try.

(4) Let me think about it.　　　　　　讓我考慮考慮。
　　Lemme think about it.

(5) Let me out!　　　　　　　　　　　放我出去！
　　Lemme out!

got it
的連音變化

🔊 078

got it → gadi

[gɑdɪ]

● got 的 [t] 因為夾在兩個母音中間，所以稍稍強化為[彈舌音 d]。

🌸 *Speak up*

. . . .

(1) I got it at the grocery store.   我在雜貨店買的。

(2) He got it from Mary.   Mary給他的。

(3) They got it last week.   他們上星期拿到的。

(4) I got it for only five dollars.   我只花五塊錢就買到了。

(5) We got it for free.   這東西是免費的。

(6) You got it?   你懂了嗎？

70 get it
的連音變化

🔊079

get it → gedi
[gɛdɪ]

● get的[t]因為夾在兩個母音中間，所以稍微強化為[彈舌音d]。

🌸 Speak up

(1) Do you get it?　　　　　　你懂嗎？

(2) We get it.　　　　　　　　我們了解。

(3) Don't get it wrong.　　　　別搞錯喔。

(4) Let's get it started.　　　　開始吧。

(5) Let's get it done.　　　　　一起完成吧。

(6) You'll get it hot and strong　你如果這樣做會被狠狠訓一
if you do this.　　　　　　頓的。

what a
的連音變化

what a → **wada**
[wɑdə]

● what 的 h 消音，[t]夾在兩個 a 之間，所以會變成輕輕的[彈舌音d]，和後面的 a 相連便形成了 wada。

 *Speak up*

....

(1) What a beautiful home run!　　真是個完美的全壘打！

(2) What a jerk!　　真是個渾蛋！

(3) What a day!　　真是糟糕的一天！

(4) What a funny story!　　真好笑的故事！

(5) What a strange lady!　　真是個奇怪的女人！

(6) What a nice man!　　真是個大好人！

72 what was
的連音變化

🔊 081

what was → **wawaz**
[wɑwɑz]

🌸 Speak up

(1) What was he up to?   他在忙什麼？

(2) What was your name again?   你的名字是什麼？我忘了。

(3) What was Jack thinking?   Jack在想什麼？

(4) What was your childhood like?   你的童年是怎樣過的？

(5) What was your mom talking about?   你媽在說什麼？

(6) What was that about?   那是什麼？

73 what are you
的連音變化

what are you
→ wadcha
[wɑdʒə]

● what 的 h 消音，are 的音完全消掉，於是what 的尾音 t 直接和弱化的 you(ya)連音，形成watcha的音（請參考第8條要訣）。又因為tch前後的母音影響，把tch[tʃ]強化為dch[dʒ]，最終成為wadcha。

🌸 *Speak up*

. . . .

(1) What are you up to?　　　　你在忙什麼？

(2) What are you thinking?　　　你在想什麼？

(3) What are you cooking?　　　你在煮什麼？

(4) What are you laughing at?　　你在笑什麼？

(5) What are you crying for?　　你在哭什麼？

(6) What are you going to do?　　你打算做什麼?

74 what happened 的連音變化

wha[t] [h]appened

→ # wadappend

[wɑdæpənd]

● what 和 happened 的 h 都消音，what 的 [t] 弱化成非常微弱的 [彈舌音 d]。若說話速度更快，有時候連 d 都會消音，而變成 wa_append。

🌸 *Speak up*

(1) What happened to him?　　　他怎麼了？

(2) What happened yesterday?　　昨天發生什麼事了？

(3) What happened to you?　　　你怎麼了？

(4) What happened is none of your business.　　不管發生什麼事都不關你的事。

(5) What happened to your foot?　　你的腳怎麼了？

(6) What happened last night?　　昨天晚上發生什麼事了？

75 pick it up
的連音變化

pick it up → **pigidap**
[pɪgɪdəp]

● pick it up會一氣呵成地唸過去，k音強化成g。it 的 t 和 what 的 t 命運相仿，後面若接母音，會弱化成非常微弱的彈舌音d。若說話速度更快，有時連 d 都會偷偷消音，而變成 pigi_ap。

🌸 *Speak up*

(1) I'll pick it up in person.   我會親自去拿。

(2) She'll pick it up this afternoon.   她今天下午會去拿。

(3) When do you want to pick it up?   你什麼時候要去拿？

(4) He'll pick it up tonight.   他今晚會去拿。

(5) Pick it up with your hands.   用手去撿。

(6) Please pick it up for me.   請幫我拿。

76 check it out
的連音變化

che**ck** **it** ou~~t~~

→ **chegidou**

[tʃɛgɪdaʊ]

🌸 *Speak up*

(1) Please check it out as soon as you can.　請盡快去看一下。

(2) Why don't you check it out on our Web site?　你為什麼不上我們的網站去看一下？

(3) I'll have to check it out before I buy it.　在我買之前，我得去查查這方面的資訊。

(4) You should check it out sometime.　你應該抽空去看一下。

(5) Check it out for yourself!　去看一下吧！

77 get out of
的連音變化

■))086

get out of

→ gedoudav
[gɛdaʊdəv]

😊 *Speak up*

(1) She's trying to get out of it by calling in sick.   她想以生病為藉口推託此事。

(2) What do you get out of it?   你從中得到什麼好處？

(3) He wants to get out of the contract.   他想要解約。

(4) I'll get out of jail tomorrow.   我明天就出獄了。

(5) Get out of my way!   走開啦！

(6) Let's get out of here!   我們趕快閃人！

78 send you
的連音變化

sen**d** **y**ou
→ **sendcha**
[sɛndʒə]

● 還記得 ~d+you 的變音嗎？請參見第 9 條要訣。

🌸 *Speak up*

. . . .

(1) They'll send you a new
model.

他們會寄給你新的型號。

(2) I'll send you a letter as soon
as possible.

我會盡快寄信給你。

(3) I'll send you a Christmas
card next year.

明年我會寄耶誕卡給你。

(4) She'll probably send you a
gift.

她可能會寄禮物給你。

(5) They'll send you a thank-
you card.

他們會寄一張感謝卡給你。

that'll
的連音變化

◀)) 088

that'll → thadle
[ðædl̩]

● t 弱化成微弱的彈舌音 d。

🌼 *Speak up*

(1) That'll be fine.   可以。

(2) That'll be $346 all together.   全部總共346元。

(3) That'll be the day!   終將有這麼一天！

(4) That'll do.   那樣可行。

(5) That'll have to wait.   需要等等看。

(6) That'll be enough.   應該是足夠的。

80 getting
的連音變化

getting

■◯))089

→ geddin'
[gɛdɪn]

● 無聲子音[t]被前後的母音包圍時，會強化變成[彈舌音d]，請參考第48條要訣。

🌸 *Speak up*

(1) Are you getting ready? 　　　　準備好了嗎？

(2) You are getting married? 　　　 你要結婚了嗎？

(3) Are you getting along with your boss? 　　你跟老闆處得來嗎？

(4) I'm getting a new computer tomorrow. 　　我明天就會得到一台新電腦了。

(5) I'm getting cold. 　　　　　　我覺得好冷。

(6) He's getting his teeth fixed today. 　　　他今天要去補牙。

(7) Right now I'm getting a haircut. 　　　我現在要去剪頭髮了。

81 ought to
的連音變化

🔊 090

ought to → oda
[ɔdə]

😊 *Speak up*

(1) You ought to see a doctor.　　　你得去看醫生。

(2) I ought to start studying.　　　我必須要開始用功了。

(3) You ought to be more polite　　你應該對別人禮貌點。
to people.

(4) You ought to make an　　　　你必須趕快約個時間才行。
appointment soon.

(5) You ought to tell your　　　　在事情還來得及補救之前，
parents before it's too late.　　你應該告訴你的爸媽。

(6) He ought to treat you better.　他得對你好一點才對。

82 kind of
的連音變化

🔊091

kind of → **kinda**
[kaɪndə]

● kind of 連音後會唸成 kinda。在發of的[v] 音時，只要門牙輕輕碰一下嘴唇即可，實際上只是停頓一下，不會真的發音。在非正式的書寫中通常會直接寫成kinda。

🌼 *Speak up*

. . . .

(1) It was kinda embarrassing.   真有點兒難為情。

(2) I kinda like him.   我有點喜歡他。

(3) She's kinda pretty, isn't she?   她蠻漂亮的，不是嗎？

(4) It's kinda hot in here.   這裡有點熱。

(5) Those cakes are kinda expensive.   那些蛋糕有點貴。

83 would you like
的連音變化

would you like → **wudchalaik**

[wʊdʒəlaɪk]

■))092

● 請參考第9條要訣。

🌸 *Speak up*

(1) Would you like some wine? 你想喝點酒嗎？

(2) Would you like some juice? 想喝點果汁嗎？

(3) Would you like to go out tonight? 今晚想外出嗎？

(4) Would you like me to drive the car for you? 你希望我幫你開車嗎？

(5) What would you like for dinner? 你晚餐想吃什麼？

(6) Would you like some sugar for your coffee? 你咖啡要加點糖嗎？

CHAPTER 7 實況對話總複習
Practice Speaking Challenge!

▼ **Karla and Chris are brother and sister. Karla tries to wake up Chris.**
Karla 和 Chris 是姊弟，Karla 正在叫 Chris 起床。

Karla: _____ guy! Why aren't you _____?

_____!

Chris: _____ a few more minutes, Karla. I'm still

tired.

Karla: _____ about? It's three in the

afternoon!

Chris: I know, but I _____ headache. It _____

hurts.

Karla: _____ help? _____ some

medicine?

Chris: _____ have? I _____ take

something

Karla: Eat this capsule. _____ with a glass of water.

Chris: _____. I could probably _____ few

more of those.

Karla: Anyway, _____ last night? _____

guess... you were drunk last night?

Chris: No, no, I wasn't drinking. I went on a first date.

Karla: Oh, _____ go on a date with? _____

nice?

Chris: Yes, so I asked her to marry me. _____

strange?

Karla: _____ you thinking! _____ her

response?

Chris: _____, she hit me on the head!

Ouch!

Karla: _____ girl! You _____ call her. She

sounds fun!

Chris: _____ my room. I'm _____ a little

annoyed.

Karla: Maybe she'll _____ get well card!

_____ nice!

Chris: Ha ha ha. Catch _____ later, sis. _____?

I _____ nap...

Answer Keys

Chapter 7 Practice Speaking Challenge!

▼ Karla and Chris are brother and sister.
Karla tries to wake up Chris.
Karla 和 Chris 是姊弟，Karla 正在叫 Chris 起床。

Karla: What a guy! Why aren't you getting up? Get out of bed!

你這男人還真好命！為什麼還不起來？趕快起床啊！

Chris: Give me a few more minutes, Karla. I'm still tired.

再給我幾分鐘，Karla。我真的很累。

Karla: What are you talking about? It's three in the afternoon!

你到底在講什麼？現在已經是下午三點了耶！

Chris: I know, but I have a headache. It kind of hurts.

我知道，但我頭很痛。

Karla: How can I help? Would you like some medicine?

需要我幫忙嗎？你要吃點藥嗎？

Chris: What do you have? I got to take something.

你有什麼藥？我的確需要一些藥來治我的頭痛。

Karla: Eat this capsule. Take it with a glass of water.

配一杯水，把這個膠囊吃了。

Chris: Got it. I could probably use a few more of those.

了解，或許我得多吃幾顆。

Karla: Anyway, what happened last night? Let me guess, you were drunk last night?

嗯，昨天發生什麼事了？讓我猜猜，你昨晚喝醉了。

Chris: No, no, I wasn't drinking. I went on a first date.

沒有，我昨天沒喝酒，我約了一個女生出去─第一次約會。

Karla: Oh, who did you go on a date with? Is she nice?

喔，你跟誰約會？對方正嗎？

Chris: Yes, so I asked her to marry me. Is that strange?

正啊，所以我就跟她求婚了。很奇怪對不對？

Karla: What were you thinking! What was her response?

你到底在想什麼！那她有什麼反應呢？

Chris: Check it out, she hit me on the head! Ouch!

你看，她海K了我的腦袋瓜一下！好痛！

Karla: What a girl! You ought to call her. She sounds fun!

這女人真猛！你應該再打個電話給她。她聽起來很有趣！

Chris: Get out of my room. I'm getting a little annoyed.

趕快滾啦。我覺得很煩。

Karla: Maybe she'll send you a get well card! That'll be nice!

或許她會寄張卡片祝你早日康復！不錯吧！

Chris: Ha ha ha. Catch ya later, sis. Got it? I need a nap...

哈哈哈，姊，我說「再見」，你懂了嗎？
我現在要睡覺了。

CHAPTER
8

實用經典表達句

現在來學學英語中的經典表達句,順便練練你的口說和聽力吧!

愛情是盲目的
Love is blind.

🔊094

Love is blind.
[lʌvɪzblaɪnd]

● love的 [v] 與is的[ɪ]子母連音。blind 的 [d] 因為是在句尾，所以會被弱化。

 *Speak up*

A: Why is she dating Andy? 為什麼她會跟 Andy 交往？
Andy is ten years older than Andy 比她大十歲耶！
her!
B: She says she would love him 她說不管 Andy 幾歲她都愛
at any age. Love is blind! 他。愛情是盲目的！

85 少管閒事！
Mind your own bussiness!

🔊 095

Mind your own business!
[maɪdʒɚ]

● mind 與 your 的連音可參考第9條要訣。

🌸 *Speak up*

A: What were you and your wife talking about? 你和你老婆在說什麼？

B: Mind your own business! 少管閒事！

86 外面下起傾盆大雨
It's raining cats and dogs.

◀》096

It's raining cats and dogs.
[kætzəndɔgz]

 *Speak up*

A: I'm going to walk to the
   store. Do you want to come?

B: You shouldn't go outside.
   It's raining cats and dogs!

我要用走的去那家店，你要一起去嗎？

還是不要出去比較好，外面雨下得很大！

87 有總比沒有好
Something is better than nothing.

◀)) 097

Something is better than nothing.
[ðænʌθɪn]

● better 的 [t] 音變成 [彈舌音d]。請參考第49條要訣。

🌸 Speak up

A: My parents sent me socks for my birthday.

我爸媽給我的生日禮物是襪子。

B: Well, something is better than nothing!

嗯，有總比什麼都沒有好！

88 我緊張到胃痛
I have butterflies in my stomach.

🔊 098

I have butterflies in my stomach.

● -tter的變音請參考第49條要訣。

😊 *Speak up*

A: I can't perform in the play tonight. I have butterflies in my stomach.

我今晚不能參與演出。我緊張到胃痛。

B: Don't be nervous. You are a great actress!

別緊張，你是個很棒的演員！

89

要就拿去，
不要就拉倒
You can take it or leave it.

🔊 99

You can take it or leave it.
[tegɪ]   [livɪ]

🌸 *Speak up*

A: Excuse me, how much is that black motor-bike?

請問一下，那台黑色的機車要多少錢？

B: Twenty thousand dollars. You can take it or leave it.

二萬元。要就拿去，不要就拉倒。

90 他有幾兩重，我都瞭若指掌
I can read him like an open book.

◀)) 100

I can read him like an
[ridɪm]   [laɪgən]
open book.

🌸 *Speak up*

....

A: How did you know that he was lying about his girlfriend.

你怎麼知道他說有女朋友這件事是在說謊。

B: I've known him since we were kids. I can read him like an open book.

我從小就認識他了，他有幾兩重，我都瞭若指掌。

91 我怕待太久
會變得不受歡迎

I don't want to wear out my welcome.

■》)) 101

I don't want to wear out my welcome.

 *Speak up*

A: I should leave now. I don't want to wear out my welcome.

我該走了，我怕待太久會變得不受歡迎。

B: Don't be silly. You can stay here as long as you like.

別說這些傻話了，你想待在這裡多久都歡迎。

92 她心不在焉
She had her head in the clouds.

🔊102

She had her head in the
[ædɚ]
clouds.

🌸 *Speak up*

A: Why was she fired?

B: She never paid attention at the meetings. She always had her head in the clouds!

她為什麼被炒魷魚？

她每次開會都不專心，老心不在焉！

93 隨你便
Suit yourself.

🔊 103

Suit yourself.
[sutʃɚsɛlf]

● 尾音t和your的連音請參考第8條要訣。

🌸 *Speak up*

A: If you don't mind, I prefer to eat in my bedroom.

B: Fine. Suit yourself. But remember to clean up.

如果你不介意的話,我想要在我房間吃東西。

好,隨你便。但要記得清乾淨。

94

幹得好！
Good for you!

◀)) 104

Good for you!

[gʊfəjə]

😊 *Speak up*

....

A: I stood up to my racist and sexist teacher today.

B: Good for you! I was always too afraid.

我今天挺身對抗我那有種族和性別歧視的老師。

幹得好！我根本沒這個膽。

 **95**

了解
Got it.

◀))105

Got it.
[gɑdɪ]

🌸 Speak up
··

A: Please don't call me after 別在三更半夜打電話給我，
   midnight. Do you 聽清楚沒？
   understand?

B: I got it. 了解。

162

96 我可不是在 跟你開玩笑！ I mean it!

◀)) 106

I mean it!
[minɪ]

😊 *Speak up*

A: Can I please borrow one thousand dollars?

可以跟你借一千元嗎？

B: Stop asking me for money. I mean it!

別再來跟我借錢了，我可沒在跟你開玩笑！

繼續保持下去
Keep it up.

🔊 107

[kibɪdəp]

🌸 *Speak up*

A: Teacher, did I pass last week's exam?

老師，我上個星期的考試有過嗎？

B: You did very well. Keep it up. I'm really proud of you.

你考得很好，繼續保持下去。我真的很以你為榮！

98 聽清楚了
Read my lips.

■)) 108

Read my lips.

🌸 *Speak up*

A: Can I borrow a hundred
dollars? I know I owe you
a lot already but I'm broke.

B: Read my lips. N-O. No!

可不可以借我一百元？我知
道我已經欠你很多了，但我
真的很窮。

聽清楚了。「不─行。」

99 用說的比較容易
Talk is cheap.

Talk is cheap.
[tɔgɪztʃip]

🌼 *Speak up*

....

A: Tomorrow I will definitely
   quit smoking.

明天我一定戒菸。

B: Talk is cheap.

用說的比較容易。

100 乞丐沒有選擇的餘地
Beggars can't be choosers.

■))110

Beggars can't be choosers.

🌸 *Speak up*

. . . .

A: I really needed a bike so I asked him, but he only had a baby's bike!

B: Well, you know what they say. Beggars can't be choosers.

我真的很需要一台腳踏車。我問過他了，但他只有兒童車。

嗯，你知道的，乞丐沒有選擇的餘地。

話別說得太早
Don't speak too soon.

🔊 111

Don't speak too soon.

[donsbi]

 *Speak up*

A: I think we won the game! There's only two minutes left!

我想我們贏定了！離比賽結束只剩兩分鐘而已！

B: Don't speak too soon. It's not over until it's over.

話別說得太早，比賽還沒真正結束之前，什麼事都很難說。

明天又是嶄新的一天
Tomorrow
is another day.

🔊112

Tomorrow is another day.

[ɪzə]

 *Speak up*

A: Today was the worst day of my life.

B: Relax tonight. Tomorrow is another day.

今天是我一生中過得最糟的一天。

今晚好好休息，明天又是嶄新的一天。

有人偷偷告訴我
A little bird told me.

🔊 113

A little bird told me.
[lɪdl̩]

🌸 *Speak up*

A: So, you're getting married. 嗯，你要結婚啦。

B: That was supposed to be a secret! How did you find out? 這應該是個秘密啊，你怎麼知道的？

A: A little bird told me. 有人偷偷告訴我的。

104 以牙還牙
An eye for an eye.

🔊 114

An eye for an eye.
[ənaɪ]　　　　　[frənaɪ]

● 這句話原本是 An eye for an eye, and a tooth for a tooth. (剛好和中文的「以牙還牙，以眼還眼」順序相反)，但因太冗長了，所以簡化為 An eye for an eye.。

 *Speak up*

A: Why did your daughter slap　為什麼你女兒今天打我女兒
   my daughter's face today?　耳光？
B: Your daughter hit her　你女兒昨天打她，所以她才
   yesterday, so an eye for　以牙還牙。
   an eye.

🔊 115

I have a sweet tooth.
[swituθ]

 Speak up

A: Every morning you are eating candy.

每天早上你總是糖不離口。

B: I can't stop. I have a sweet tooth.

我真的沒辦法戒掉，我太愛甜食了。

我真的不知道
I haven't got a clue.

🔊 116

I haven't got a clue.
[gɑdə]

🌸 *Speak up*

A: Do you know what time the train is coming?

你知道火車什麼時候會到嗎？

B: I haven't got a clue. The train is always late.

我真的不知道。火車總是誤點。

107 這簡單得很
It's a piece of cake.

◀)) 117

It's a piece of cake.
[ɪzə]　　　　　　　[pɪsə]

🌼 Speak up

A: Are you sure you can fix my computer?

你確定能把我的電腦修好嗎？

B: I've used computers for ten years. For me it's a piece of cake.

我已經用了十年的電腦，修理對我來說是輕而易舉的事。

108 聽我的準沒錯
Take my word for it.

🔊 118

Take my word for it.
[temaɪ]

😊 *Speak up*

A: Are you sure your uncle would like a surprise party?

B: Take my word for it. My uncle loves surprises.

你確定你舅舅會喜歡驚喜派對嗎？

聽我的準沒錯，我舅舅超愛驚喜的。

109

我完全同意
You can say that again.

You can say that again.

[ðædəgɛn]

🌸 *Speak up*

A: This fish tastes really good. Your father is a great cook.

這魚真的好好吃喔，你爸的廚藝真棒。

B: You can say that again. Actually, he's a professional.

我完全同意。事實上，他是烹調專家。

可以改天嗎？
Can I take a rainckeck?

🔊 120

Can I take a raincheck?
[tegə]

🌸 *Speak up*

A: Would you like to come to my house for dinner?

你要來我家吃晚餐嗎？

B: I can't today. Can I take a raincheck?

今天不行耶。可以改天嗎？

我真是受夠他了
I'm so fed up with him.

🔊 121

I'm so fed up with him.
[fɛdʌ]   [wɪθɪm]

🐸 *Speak up*

A: Why did you tell him to find another place to live?

為什麼你要他搬走？

B: I'm so fed up with him. He never cleans up after himself!

我真是受夠他了，他每次東西用完之後都不清理！

112 有些事還是
不要說的好
Some things are
better left unsaid.

🔊 122

Some things are better
left unsaid.

[lɛfdʌnsɛd]

🌸 Speak up

A: Why didn't you tell me you
were angry?

為什麼你不告訴我你在生氣？

B: Some things are better left
unsaid.

有些事情還是不要說的好。

I DON'T WANNA LOZCHA.

MEMO

掌握 8 大發音要訣！：英語聽說超流暢 / Tim Stone 著 .
-- 初版 . -- 臺北市：笛藤 , 2020.10
　　面；　公分
ISBN 978-957-710-799-2(平裝)

1. 英語 2. 發音

805.141　　　　　109015576

2020 年 10 月 23 日　初版第 1 刷　定價 240 元

編著／Tim Stone

編輯／羅金純・伍曉玥・葉艾青

封面設計／王舒玗

內頁設計／CP（李靜屏）

總編輯／賴巧凌

編輯企劃／笛藤出版

發行所／八方出版股份有限公司

發行人／林建仲

地址／台北市中山區長安東路二段 171 號 3 樓 3 室

電話／ (02) 2777-3682

傳真／ (02) 2777-3672

總經銷／聯合發行股份有限公司

地址／新北市新店區寶橋路 235 巷 6 弄 6 號 2 樓

電話／ (02)2917-8022・(02)2917-8042

製版廠／造極彩色印刷製版股份有限公司

地址／新北市中和區中山路二段 380 巷 7 號 1 樓

電話／ (02)2240-0333・(02)2248-3904

郵撥帳戶／八方出版股份有限公司

郵撥帳號／19809050